Surprise Attack

Dan held his finger on the trigger of the Sharps, cocked the hammer and took careful aim. When the Sharps roared the whole thicket of mesquite responded, leaping into life with the crash of rifles.

There was wild confusion in the arroyo. From both arroyo and mesquite the yells arose. A savage, wiry and swift as a cat, scrambled up the opposite bank, poised for a moment and then collapsed into a bundle of rags and brown flesh. From the mesquite, heedless of thorns or footing, the herders came leaping, whooping, savage as the Apaches themselves. Dan Shea dropped the Sharps and with his pistol in hand crashed through the growth and ran into the fray.

Range of
Holden
Hoofs

John Trace

LEISURE BOOKS NEW YORK CITY

To Dr. G. W. R. Smith

A LEISURE BOOK®

July 2009

Published by special arrangement with Golden West Literary Agency.

Dorchester Publishing Co., Inc.
200 Madison Avenue
New York, NY 10016

ISBN 10: 0-8439-6280-1
ISBN 13: 978-0-8439-6280-2
E-ISBN: 978-1-4285-0706-7

The name "Leisure Books" and the stylized "L" with design are trademarks of Dorchester Publishing Co., Inc.

Printed in the United States of America.

10 9 8 7 6 5 4 3 2 1

Visit us on the web at www.dorchesterpub.com.

El pie de la oveja siempre déjà oro.

Wherever the sheep sets his hoof, there gold is found.

SPANISH PROVERB

CHAPTER ONE:

COLD DECK

At noon, well along the road to Bendición, the El Paso stage stopped to change horses. Since early morning Dan Shea had been riding the leather-covered seat, and here at the nooning he stepped out to stretch his long legs. Fitzpatrick, the saloon-keeper, also alighted from the stage, correcting the angle of his narrow-brimmed derby hat and settling his coat more truly on his shoulders.

The trip down had been a pleasant one despite the heat which comes early in the middle valley of the Rio Grande. The men had enjoyed it. Fitzpatrick, returning to Bendición following a buying trip to the pueblo of Albuquerque, was a friendly, talk-ative man, his occupation, his identity and his convictions an open book for all to read. Dan Shea, more reticent, had risen a trifle to Fitzpatrick's talk, and a mutual and common meeting ground brought them together. At the Vicksburg siege Dan Shea had been outside the city; Fitzpatrick within it. Old enemies, their animosity had long since died. The Lost Cause was lost. As a loser, Fitzpatrick had the tale of many a victory to recount. As a winner, Dan Shea could afford to be generous. The bitterness of the fight was gone from between these fighting men, and here in the middle of the New Mexico Territory the war was a remote thing, as far distant as a game of chess played ten years agone.

"Yank an' Reb," Fitzpatrick said, leading the way toward the dark door of the stage station, "an' both of us Irish. It just goes to show what an Irishman will do to get into a fight. I'll buy you a drink, Shea."

"And I'll buy your dinner," Dan Shea answered. "We lay over here."

As they entered the station Fitzpatrick pushed back his hat. He was a lank man, sandy haired, hair and mustache the color of the desert, and his eyes a faded blue. Dan Shea, following his acquaintance, was heavier, broader and more youthful. Black Irish showed in hair and blue eyes that alertly scanned the interior of the stage stop.

Beside the desk that immediately confronted the door the bar of the stage stop stretched to the left. To the right was the dining room, the walls white plastered and the single long table almost filling the narrow space. The station manager was outside with the hostlers, and only a native barman attended the bar, while at the table three men stopped their eating to survey the newcomers. Fitzpatrick leaned easily against the bar and spoke to the barman whom he knew. Dan Shea, pausing just inside the door, scanned the room and its occupants.

The men at the table fell to eating again and Fitzpatrick said: "Give me whisky, Carlos," and looked toward Dan, lifting his eyebrows in inquiry.

"The same," Dan agreed and took the short two steps that brought him to Fitzpatrick's side. As the small glasses were set out and the bartender reached for the bottle on the back bar, there came the rattle and clank, the thudding of hoofs, that spoke the arrival of another stage. Again the men at the table lifted their heads to watch the door.

"The eastbound stage," Fitzpatrick commented. "Well"—he turned his small glass between his fingers—"I'll give you a toast, Shea: To the friends we'll see no more."

Dan Shea drank. The whisky was hot in mouth and throat, and the water that followed it was luke-warm and insipid. Replacing his glass on the bar top, he listened to the men outside. Fitzpatrick, hav-ing taken his drink, had replaced his glass and turned so that his back was to the bar and his face to the door.

"The off leader's lame," a hoarse voice said. "Picked up a stone, I reckon."

At the table the three men, finished with their meal, had risen. Now they moved, edging along the table until they reached its end, and stopped. Rough men, bearded, booted, each armed, they gathered at the table end and stood between the bar and the table, facing the door. The door darkened and the station manager filled it, his head turned so that he talked over his shoulder to a man outside.

"There's no express," the manager said and came on in, walking around the end of his desk and paus-ing behind it. "I've got a sack of mail though."

The stage guard, a stranger to Dan Shea, followed the manager, crossing to the desk and pausing be-fore it, his back to the door. He leaned his elbows on the desk, and then for a third time the doorway darkened.

Dan Shea had observed these things, not with interest but as a habit. He saw the man in the door, small, neatly dressed. The new arrival looked

quickly to right and left with beady black eyes. A
wisp of black mustache beneath his long nose completed so apparent a likeness that Dan Shea almost
laughed. Here was a mouse: one of those small,
indefinite people who cling to the side of buildings
as they walk, ready, always, to seek safety in a hole.
The man took a step from the doorway and at the
table one of the three diners said: "That's him."

Instantly Dan Shea turned. At the end of the
table the three men had gone into action. Their
weapons were in their hands, and even as Dan
looked toward them the little room rocked with the
reverberation of the shots. At the door the mousy
man staggered back, one small claw of a hand coming up as though it could ward off the heavy lead
that jerked and tugged and slammed into his slight
body. Fitzpatrick had leaped away and was crouched
against the wall, and Dan Shea, staring at the falling man beside the door, became aware that the
direction of fire had changed and that he himself
was in the center of it. On the bar the whisky bottle
broke and the liquor splashed, and Fitzpatrick was
yelling: "Down, Shea. Get down!"

Dan dropped to his knees. His own weapon kicked
sharply into the fork of his hand, and the smell of
smoke was sharp and acrid in his nostrils. The little
man lay beside the door and the three murderers
were running, almost trampling the body in their
haste. Fitzpatrick brushed against Dan, upsetting
him as he made for the vacant doorway, and Dan,
regaining his feet, followed toward the square of
light.

Just outside the door Fitzpatrick crouched, his
left arm raised, a long black gun leveled across it.
Toward the corral there was a hitching rack, and at

it horses milled as men mounted. Fitzpatrick fired once and then again. Dan Shea raised his own weapon and took careful sight.

Above the sharp ridge of the foresight a figure appeared momentarily. Shea's gun bounced and settled, bounced again, and on his horse a man lurched forward, clutching at the saddle. Then horses and men were gone, wheeling sharply about the end of the adobe-walled corral, and Dan Shea lowered his gun. Fitzpatrick had straightened and was standing just beyond Dan, staring at the corner of the corral. For perhaps a full minute he stood there and then, turning, looked at Dan Shea.

"You hit one that last shot," Fitzpatrick said almost casually. "Looked like you hurt him bad."

Dan's mouth was dry, his tongue seeming to cling to its roof. "They were waiting for him," he said thickly.

"Sure they were." Fitzpatrick's voice was gruff. "He never had a chance. Came through the door and walked right into it. Well . . . ?"

They turned then, acting on common impulse, and went back into the station. The mousy man lay beside the door, just where he had fallen. The station manager was bending over him, and the shotgun guard and the driver stood staring down. Over by the table two women hovered: the cook and the waitress. The waitress had picked up a soiled dish and was holding it. As Dan Shea came through the door the driver said: "He was goin' to Albuquerque. That's all I know."

"They got away," Fitzpatrick announced, replacing his weapon in its holster under his coat. "My pardner here hit one when they went around the corner of the corral."

Dan was suddenly aware of his own gun, heavy in his hand. He lifted it, sliding it down into place beneath his arm. Over behind the bar the native bartender showed the round moon of his face as he came up from hiding, and the station manager, rising, made an unnecessary statement.

"He's dead."

The waitress dropped her plate, screamed and threw her apron up over her head, turning blindly and banging against the table as she made toward the kitchen door. Behind Dan Shea men arrived: the driver of the El Paso stage, the guard and the hostlers. They pushed Dan aside, their hands rough and their voices hoarse as they asked questions. The stationman looked at them.

"I don't know," he said. "I don't know just what happened. I was gettin' the mail sack for Charlie when it started."

"He walked in and they just went to shootin'," Fitzpatrick stated. "Just like that."

Dan looked at the man on the floor. He was a dead mouse now, an inoffensive, harmless, little dead animal. The black mustache was very dark above his lip and the beady eyes had lost all their sharpness.

"I don't know who they were," the station manager said, answering a question. "They just came in an' ordered dinner. I don't know who they were."

The guard of the westbound stage, the drivers, the hostlers, the eastbound messenger who had been at the desk, even the station manager who had stooped for the mailbag, were filled with questions. The drivers and the hostlers had been in the corral when they heard the shots. Wisely they had remained behind the protection of the thick adobe walls. They had not seen what happened, either inside or outside the station. As always, in aftermath, each man spoke, identifying his part in this tragedy, placing himself as to time and location during its occurrence, so filled with his own small part that it became of pre-eminent importance in his recital. Dan Shea leaned against the wall, not looking at the dead man but watching the others, tension easing out of him. Fitzpatrick, too, was relaxing. He answered the questions that poured in upon him, his words brief, sharp, terse. No one could identify the men who had been at the table. No one could identify the dead man.

"His grip's on the coach," the eastbound driver said. "I'll get it." He went out.

"No," Fitzpatrick answered a hostler's question, "we weren't with him. We're headed west. We just came in for a drink and to eat dinner."

The driver came back lugging a heavy telescope grip. He dumped it down on the floor. "You think we ought to open it?" he asked doubtfully.

"The sheriff 'll open it," the station manager answered. "You get hold of him as soon as you get to Bendición, Bill. Tell him what happened."

"What are you goin' to do with him?" The driver gestured to the body. "You want me to take him in?"

The stageman shook his head. "We'll keep him for the sheriff," he answered. "Juan, you an' Lucero get him out. Take him down to the feed room an' wrap him in a tarp. Fitz, you'll tell the sheriff when you get to town. You an' this gentleman seen it all, didn't you?" His eyes sought Dan Shea.

Dan nodded. The hostlers were lifting the body, one at the head, the other at the feet. Dan moved aside to give them passageway.

"The stage company ain't responsible," the stationman stated. "You know that? You saw what happened?"

"We'll tell Youtsey all about it," Fitzpatrick agreed. He had joined Dan and was standing beside him.

The station manager was brisk. "You gents certainly took a hand," he commended. "They shot at you too. Smashed a bottle right beside you." He looked at Dan Shea. "Well . . . we'll get the teams changed. You want some dinner?"

Dan Shea shook his head. Fitzpatrick said, "No," and then in a drawling voice: "I've kind of lost my appetite."

The westbound driver was tugging at one heavy glove. "Get the teams changed," he rasped. "I don't want no dinner neither. We'll go on."

Dan Shea took his eyes from the little pool of blood that the mousy man had left on the floor. He looked at Fitzpatrick.

"A hell of a thing," Fitzpatrick said. "Wasn't it a hell of a thing?"

In the stage, the coach rocking on the thick leather of the thorough braces, Dan Shea and Fitzpatrick were silent. They looked out the window as the road turned, watching the stage station, its few trees, the long adobe walls of the corrals dwindle and become a child's plaything in the distance. When the road turned again and the station was gone from sight they sat, each staring moodily at the feet of the other. Atop the coach the driver, the messenger seated beside him, spoke to his teams, urging them along, finding relief in his accustomed business. Dan Shea and Fitzpatrick were denied that relief.

The coach lurched down into a wash and climbed out of it. Methodically, as though he had just found something to do, Fitzpatrick produced his long weapon from its holster, looked at it a moment and then placing the hammer at half cock, opened the loading gate and pushed out four spent shells. The empty cartridge cases tinkled as they fell to the floor of the stage. From his belt Fitzpatrick refilled the cylinder.

Dan Shea, reaching under his coat, performed a like service for his own shorter gun. Fitzpatrick dandled his weapon between his knees and, lifting his eyes from it, looked at Dan.

"Happened quick," Fitzpatrick commented.

"It did," Dan agreed.

"I missed every shot." The saloon man looked down at his gun again. "You were in line with me when it started."

Dan made no answer. After a long interval Fitzpatrick spoke again. "They must have wanted him bad."

"Bad," Dan assented.

"He never knew what happened."

"No."

Fitzpatrick shrugged and put away his gun. "You ain't a bad kind to have along," he praised. "You started quick."

"They took a shot or two at us."

Silence in the coach for a moment, broken only by the sounds of the trotting horses and the rattle of the wheels.

"I wonder why they wanted him," Fitzpatrick mused. "He didn't look like the kind that gets in trouble, did he?"

"No, he didn't."

Across from Dan, Fitzpatrick straightened his shoulders. "I don't like to get mixed up in a thing like that," he announced. "I run a good, peaceful place in Bendición. Trouble is bad for my business."

"Any kind of business," Dan amended. "Well . . . the sheriff will ask questions."

"An' we'll answer 'em," Fitzpatrick said. He was quiet for a moment, absorbed in his thoughts, then his eyes met Dan's.

"As cold a deck as was ever dealt," Fitzpatrick rasped. "He never had a chance."

"No," Dan Shea agreed slowly. "He didn't. He surely didn't."

CHAPTER TWO:
BLACK SHEEP RETURNS

Bendición was built about a plaza shaded by tower-ing cottonwoods, their leaves small green elf ears. About the plaza brown adobes squatted, and over-towering the adobes and the plaza but not of them a twin-spired mission raised its crosses skyward. At a corner of the square, not on the plaza itself but withdrawn from it, was a courthouse, and an *acequia* gurgled pleasantly beneath a bridge, bring-ing water to the cottonwoods and to the grass of the enclosure. Evening had brought surcease from the heat and brilliant sunlight of the day, and here and there beneath the awnings that porched the adobes a lamp glowed yellow and pleasant.

Dan Shea—the dust of travel removed and a hearty supper past—issued from the hotel upon the street and looked to right and left before choosing his course. He had, since his arrival, spent a good deal of time at the courthouse where with Fitzpat-rick he had informed the sheriff of the happenings at the San Felice stage station. It was evident dur-ing that period that Fitzpatrick and Youtsey, the officer, were not on good terms. Leaving the court-house, Fitzpatrick had explained briefly: "I was against him for sheriff last election."

Now, with evening all about, Dan stood in Bendición's plaza and glanced up at the light-burnished sky, at the cottonwoods and at the twin spires; then, turning deliberately, he walked along the street.

Fitzpatrick's saloon carried his name above the door. Dan went in, pausing after he had entered and surveying the room. The saloon was not pretentious. There were many other places along Bendición's dusty plaza that vaunted more and brighter lights, louder voices and greater size. Bendición drew her substance from the mines in the hills to the west, from the little farms along the river and from the stock country north and east. An odd conglomeration of a town, Bendición could afford amusement of any caliber, goods of almost any kind. Fitzpatrick's saloon plainly catered to a quiet trade. There was a bar along one side of the room, a back bar liberally stocked with glasses and bottled goods and, beyond the bar, three tables. Fitzpatrick, coat gone now and vest hanging open, came from the bar to greet Dan Shea at the door.

After the greeting Dan was introduced to Fitzpatrick's bartender, and then the two men seated themselves at a table. The bartender, assured that it was too soon after supper for a drink, returned to his post and Fitzpatrick, leaning back in his chair, surveyed his companion.

"They treat you all right at the hotel?" he asked.

Dan nodded, and Fitzpatrick, finding a cigar, proffered it, bit the end from another and scratched a sulphur match against his boot sole. "How do you like Bendición?" he questioned around the cigar. "Pretty good town?"

"A pretty good town," Dan agreed.

Men drifted into the saloon: two townsmen who stood at the bar and ordered beer; three men—riders, cowmen from their dress—came through the door and paused at the end of the bar. The bartender went to them, attending to their wants, and Dan Shea puffed his good Havana and let the smoke trail up.

"A pretty good town," he said again.

"Halfway between Albuquerque an' El Paso," Fitzpatrick stated. "There's lots of minin'. It would be a good town to settle in." He looked narrowly at his companion.

"I . . ." Dan began and checked.

Sam Youtsey, the sheriff, had come through the door and, nodding briefly to the cowboys at the bar end, advanced toward the table.

Youtsey stopped beside Shea and Fitzpatrick, pulled out a chair and sat down. "I sent a wagon out for the body," the sheriff announced without preamble. "It ought to be in tomorrow."

Fitzpatrick nodded gravely, and Dan inched his chair around so that he more fully faced the officer. The sheriff looked at Dan Shea. "What's your business here, Mr Shea?" he asked bluntly.

Dan was slow in replying. The question broke the ethics of the time and country. A man's business was private until he chose to announce it. Still, the interest of the sheriff was official rather than personal.

"I'm looking for some sheep that can be bought reasonably," Dan said. "You know of any?"

Youtsey thought a moment before replying. "Sheep?" he said when he spoke.

"I said sheep."

Youtsey looked at Fitzpatrick and seemed to smile. "You don't look like a sheepman," he commented, turning back to Dan.

"But sheep are what I'm interested in." Dan lifted his eyes from the sheriff. At the bar the cowboys were listening. Youtsey shifted in his chair.

"Figgerin' to locate?" he asked.

"I just want to buy some sheep," Dan drawled.

"Well"—Youtsey's admission was grudging—"there's some sheep in the country. I could spare 'em, I guess, if you wanted to take 'em out." He grinned appreciatively at his little joke. "The La Luz folks got some, an' you might find some sheep at El Puerto del Sol. Don Martin O'Connor might let you have some."

"Don Martin O'Connor?" Dan echoed the words.

"That's his name," Youtsey said. "He owns El Puerto del Sol. Yeah . . . I guess you could find some sheep there."

"Whereabouts is it?" Dan leaned forward.

"East." The sheriff waved a vague hand. "Mail hack goes out there. O'connor's headquarters are on the star route."

"When does the hack leave?"

"Tomorrow." The sheriff paused. "We're goin' to hold an inquest tomorrow mornin' too. I came to tell you. About eight o'clock. You be there." He included Fitzpatrick in his glance. The saloonkeeper nodded.

"At the courthouse," Youtsey added and stood up. He nodded to Fitzpatrick, glanced at Dan and then, turning, walked toward the door, stopping to speak briefly to the cowmen at the bar.

When Youtsey was gone Fitzpatrick grunted. "The sheriff," he drawled, "is quite a joker."

"How do you mean?" Dan asked.

Fitzpatrick did not answer that question. "Why didn't you tell me you wanted to buy some sheep?" he asked. "I could have steered you."

"I came down tonight to talk to you about it." Dan Shea smiled.

"Oh!" Fitzpatrick's grunt was mollified.

"Do you," Dan spoke slowly, "think I might pick up some sheep from O'Connor?"

Fitzpatrick's eyes narrowed in thought. "Don Martin," he drawled, "is a pretty hard citizen. Nobody around here likes him much. There's other places where you might get sheep easier."

"But O'Connor's got 'em?"

"He's got plenty." The saloonkeeper broke off and appeared to be lost in thought. "Why don't you try someplace else?" he asked suddenly. "O'Connor . . ." Fitzpatrick broke off abruptly.

"It's the closest place, I take it," Dan answered. "What I want is sheep. I'm not interested in the kind of man I get 'em from."

Up at the end of the bar one of the cowpunchers spoke, lifting his voice until the words were plain. "Let's git out of here. I never could stand the smell of a lousy sheepman."

Dan Shea flushed. Fitzpatrick lifted his head and looked at the speaker, his stare long and slow and hard.

"If I bother your business . . ." Dan began, shifting as though to rise.

"Set still," Fitzpatrick rasped, continuing to stare at the men.

"It does kinda stink in here." Another of the three made his ideas evident.

Fitzpatrick got up. "Get out then," he said definitely. "Down at the honky-tonk's where you belong. Go on down there!" The saloon man's voice was hard, rasping. Dan Shea had seen Fitzpatrick in action. Fitzpatrick, he judged, was a pretty salty citizen, a man capable of looking after things.

"Go on!" Fitzpatrick ordered curtly.

At the end of the bar the cowboys hesitated. They had been drinking, were drunk enough to be ugly. Fitzpatrick moved away from the table and took a step. One of the cowboys put money on the bar.

"It'll be a damned long time before we're back," he snapped, glaring at Fitzpatrick.

"It won't be half long enough!" Fitzpatrick rasped.

The cowboys went out, one of them clinking change defiantly in his hand. Fitzpatrick sat down. "I've been wantin' to do that," he drawled.

Dan made no comment. There was something between Fitzpatrick and the men who had gone out, some old quarrel half settled.

"Have a glass of beer," Fitzpatrick invited.

The bartender brought the beer. Dan and Fitzpatrick sat drinking it, sipping slowly. The beer was not quite warm, not quite cold. "I can't get ice in here," Fitzpatrick said. "Have to keep the beer in the cellar."

Dan nodded.

The evening business had begun. Men filtered into the saloon, stepping up to the bar, speaking to Fitzpatrick, asking him concerning his trip. Dan Shea sat at the table, his fingers touching his beer glass, watching the men, watching Fitzpatrick. There was more to Fitzpatrick, he estimated, than there was to the ordinary run of saloonkeepers. Dan liked the man, realizing the force that lay under the sandy exterior, recognizing the man's strength. Fitzpatrick, he thought idly, would do to take along. He would make a hand.

"You didn't tell Youtsey that you wanted to locate here," Fitzpatrick said suddenly.

"I don't, really," Dan answered. "I want to trail sheep north. There's a market in Colorado. I need to make a little money. The panic wiped me out."

"It's made hard times every place," Fitzpatrick agreed. "I . . ." He stopped. Dan Shea was looking toward the door, his face set in harsh, hard lines.

Two newcomers were in the doorway, poised there, filling the opening. One was short, broad, with flaxen yellow hair and a blond mustache. The other, taller and dark, was plainly a native. Dan Shea stared at the blond man.

"You know him?" Fitzpatrick asked curiously.

"I know him!" Dan Shea answered shortly.

In his mind was recollection. There was heat and the hard, sharp sounds of battle all about him. Brush surrounded him, too, lying in a tangle all about, and beside Dan sprawled a man in a blue uniform: Ashland Davies, his friend. Davies was bleeding out his life. For the moment Dan Shea was back in the wilderness fight. He could almost smell the powder smoke.

"I take it you don't like Delaney," Fitzpatrick drawled.

Dan did not answer. Delaney and his companion had left the door and were coming toward the table. Delaney was looking at Fitzpatrick. His eyes left the saloonkeeper's gaze and met Dan Shea's. For an instant George Delaney stopped short, then a smile broke across his face and he came on, his hand outstretched.

"Dan Shea!" All the warmth of greeting was in

Delaney's voice. "I never thought I'd see you here. I never expected to see you again!"

Dan did not move. He ignored the outstretched hand, and his eyes, meeting Delaney's, bit into them.

"You never expected to see me anyplace, Delaney," he rapped out. "Not after you'd left me to die!"

Delaney had stopped beside the table. He lowered his hand slowly. "Why, Dan . . ." Delaney began.

Dan Shea read the bitter indictment that was in his mind. "You pulled out! You knew that Davies was dying and you knew that I was hurt. You heard me call you and you never came back. You damned coward!"

Delaney's eyes would not meet Dan's own. Dan Shea went on, his voice passionless. "Davies died. I spent the next six months in a hospital. I looked for you after I got out. I wanted to tell you what kind of a skunk you are, Delaney!"

A hot flush suffused George Delaney's cheeks. "I didn't hear you call," he evaded. "I . . ."

"That's a lie!" Dan Shea said flatly and waited.

The color drained slowly from Delaney's face. For an instant he remained, confronting Dan Shea, and then he wavered, half turning toward the bar. The native with him took a half step and glared down at Dan, his eyes hostile. "Señor . . ." he began.

"You're in poor company," Dan Shea said coldly and looked at Delaney again. Delaney completed his turn. He said: "Come on, Ramon," over his shoulder, and without a backward glance started to the door. The native paused, undecided, then wheeling swiftly, followed Delaney. The barroom was quiet until they had gone out, remained quiet. Dan let his shoulders relax until they touched the back of his chair.

"You said you knew him," Fitzpatrick drawled. "I take it he knew you, too. All right. We'll have another drink over here."

Dan shook his head. "I'll get out," he said thickly. "I'm going back to the hotel." He rose wearily to his feet. Fitzpatrick looked at the bartender who had moved to serve them.

"Let the drink go," he instructed. "I'll walk back to the hotel with you, Shea."

Outside the saloon the street was quiet enough. A wind was rustling the little leaves of the plaza's cottonwoods. Dan Shea, walking toward the hotel, Fitzpatrick beside him, hardly heard the wind. His mind was still filled with the cold anger that possessed him. Fitzpatrick strolled along, unhurried, and perforce Dan's gait matched that of his companion.

"Want to talk about it?" Fitzpatrick asked.

Words broke from Dan Shea, rushing over the dam of his mind. "He left the best friend I ever had to die! It was in the Battle of the Wilderness an' we were trapped. I couldn't get Davies out alone. I called to Delaney . . ."

"An' he never looked back," Fitzpatrick drawled. "I've thought there was somethin' wrong with George Delaney."

"I said I'd kill him!" Dan did not heed Fitzpatrick's interpolation. "I swore I'd kill him if I saw him again."

Fitzpatrick's drawl was soothing. "You couldn't do it."

Dan Shea stopped short in his stride. "I swore I would," he countered. "I swore I'd kill him."

Fitzpatrick's level voice blended with the murmur of the wind. "You couldn't do it," he repeated. "You ain't the kind of man that can do a killin'. I know you've got guts, Shea, but you ain't the kind that can step out an' drop a man cold. He's got to fight back."

They resumed their walking, Dan Shea moodily silent. A corner was turned, a street crossed, and they were almost at the hotel.

"You didn't do Delaney any good," Fitzpatrick said. "You didn't help him none. The talk will be all around town."

Still Dan said nothing. Fitzpatrick spoke again. "An' you didn't help your business any. That fello' with Delaney was Ramon de la Luz. Delaney does some business for Ramon an' they're pretty thick. I guess you won't get any De la Luz sheep, Shea."

The saloon man pondered a moment. They had stopped in front of the hotel now. "Most folks," he drawled, "like Delaney. He's got a pretty good business here. Does some law work an' sells some land, an' so on."

"Everybody always liked him," Dan said shortly.

"Until they found out about him, huh?" Fitzpatrick commented. "Well . . . good night, Shea."

"Good night," Dan Shea answered and entered the hotel.

CHAPTER THREE:
EL PUERTO DEL SOL

The Mail Hack for the East left Bendición at noon. Dan Shea, climbing into the spring wagon beside the driver, felt the fierce heat of the morning sun even in the semishade of the plaza. He had spent the morning at the courthouse, listening to Youtsey and Bendición's justice of the peace conduct an inquest, and he was glad now to have that experience behind him.

The little man who had been killed at the San Felice stage station was named Maples. So much had been ascertained from the letters found in his pocket. Other identification, there was none. The letters had come from the East, one from Boston, another from a town in Vermont, and were addressed to Sante Fe. Their contents shed no light on Maples, his connections or his business. One, apparently, came from a relative. It was signed, "Lovingly, Aunt Cora," but aside from the postmark there was no address. The other letter, from Boston, was evidently a reply to some request Maples had made. It quoted prices on suits.

The manager of the stage station who had come in for the inquest was apologetic concerning Maples' telescope grip. "That damned Lucero," the manager said, "sloped with it."

Lucero, the manager further stated, was a half-breed Mescalero Apache. He had been hired as a hostler at San Felice. Aside from that the manager knew nothing of Lucero's antecedents or of where he had gone. "Them Indians," the stageman informed, "will take anything that ain't nailed down. I guess Lucero seen the clothes an' truck in that grip an' figgered that he wanted 'em. Anyhow, he pulled out with it sometime last night."

Youtsey opened his mind concerning the slackness at the station, letting the stationman know just what he thought of such carelessness, but there was nothing that the sheriff could do about it. The grip was gone.

Fitzpatrick had come down to the post office to see Dan off. He stood leaning on the wheel beside Dan while the driver attended to those last-minute details that seem always to be a part of any departure. Dan, comfortable on the seat, his coat removed and folded beside him, settled his hat so that it shaded his eyes, and grinned down at the saloon man.

"I'll be back," he assured. "Tomorrow or the next day. I'll see what there is at El Puerto del Sol and if I don't find what I want I'll come right back here."

Fitzpatrick nodded, his blue eyes gloomy. "They're goin' to bury Maples this afternoon," he said. "He won't keep in this weather, an' I guess they've got to bury him right away, but it kind of seems a shame somehow."

"Youtsey," Dan commented dryly, "don't seem to be much stirred up over a murder. He's taking it pretty easy, it seems to me. Well, we did what we could, anyhow. We're not officers."

"No," Fitzpatrick agreed. "We ain't. Here comes the driver. You take care of yourself, Shea. I'll be lookin' for you back."

They gripped hands briefly, and Fitzpatrick retreated to the front of the post office while the driver climbed into the seat and gathered up the lines. Under his urging the horses eased into the collars and the spring wagon rolled away. When Dan looked back Fitzpatrick was still beside the post office, leaning against the wall, a solitary, inscrutable figure.

Pulling out of Bendición, the mail wagon came to the long wooden bridge that stretched across the Rio Grande. The horses' feet thumped on the planking, and the wheels rumbled. Beyond the bridge was the desert, and the road climbed slowly toward a mesa top. On either side of the road the country stretched away, rock and sand dotted with the hardy desert growths, and behind them the river lay, a green flanked serpent in the brown earth. Cat's-claw, mesquite, greasewood lined the road, here and there interspersed with sparse grass. The sun beat down and the horses walked steadily.

"Goin' to El Puerto del Sol?" the driver asked.

Dan nodded.

"Goin' to buy some sheep?"

It was apparent that Dan's business had been bruited about the town that morning. Dan nodded again.

"Ol' Don Martin ain't apt to sell you any," the driver stated and spat expertly over a wheel.

"Why not?"

"Because he ain't." A brief pause, then: "He don't sell to nobody around here."

Dan waited. Apparently the driver was going to pass out information. The driver did. "Don Martin O'Connor," he drawled. "He married one of the Alarid girls. That's how come him to have El Puerto."

"Whereabouts is it?" Dan asked.

"Right ahead," the driver answered. "We'll be on grant land pretty quick. El Puerto del Sol reaches from back of the Alforjas clear down to Alamo Creek. Soon as we cross the creek we're on Don Martin's land."

"It's an old Spanish grant?" Dan asked.

"Older 'n the hills. The Alarids have had it ever since the year one."

"It takes in lots of country?"

"From Point of Rocks on south to the Pope's Nose." Again the driver pointed with his whip. "I don't know how many acres. Neither does anybody else." The driver paused a moment and spat, then continued: "It used to take in more country, but O'Connor sold the north end to the YH outfit. They run cattle. Louder an' O'Connor been fightin' ever since Louder bought the land."

"So?" Dan pried for more information.

"Yeah. Nobody gets along with O'Connor except the *paisanos* that work for him. He's meaner 'n a damned snake."

There was a contemplative pause, and then the driver spoke again. "I got to hand it to him, though: he's kept El Puerto del Sol together. The Alarids was about to lose it. O'Connor got the place on its feet when he made that sale."

For a little time the wagon rolled along in silence. Dan Shea was thinking about the information he had received. O'Connor, from all that Dan had heard, bore a bad reputation. Perhaps Dan had been wiser to attempt his purchase at some other source. As though sensing the thought, the driver said: "He'll treat you all right. The ol' man's a gentleman. He's just tough to do business with."

"What time will we get in?" Shea asked after a time.

"Along sometime this evenin'. I lay over at El Puerto tonight an' come back tomorrow. There's another driver takes the mail on East. Hot today, ain't it?"

Dan nodded his agreement, and the driver lapsed into silence. The wagon rolled steadily ahead toward the hills that the driver had called the "Alforjas." As though reading Dan's thoughts the driver said: "Some call 'em the Packsaddle Mountains."

"Uh-huh," said Dan Shea.

Again the silence possessed them. The horses finished a climb, paused at the top to breathe and then began a descent. Below them a creek stretched away to north and south, curving, at the south, toward the Rio Grande.

"Alamo Creek," the driver announced needlessly. The tall cottonwoods along the creek had disclosed its identity.

They finished the descent, gravity striving against the dragging brake and the weight of the horses against the neckyoke. In the stream the team stood and drank, and Dan Shea, climbing down, refreshed himself upstream from the animals. When man and horses had finished the journey resumed.

"Grant land now," the driver informed.

The country seemed lifeless. Now and again a lizard ran scurrying across the road. Once a chaparral cock, *el paisano* to the natives, appeared, his wings half spread as he ran along ahead of the team.

"They always want a race," the driver drawled. "Them road runners can cover country fast as a horse."

Dan nodded and watched the bird until it darted from the road into mesquite. "Kill snakes too," the driver said, speaking of the road runner.

Behind them the sun lowered toward the west. Their shadows marched before them, growing longer and more gaunt. The driver took a fresh chew and proffered Dan the plug. "Some folks," he drawled, still speaking of the bird, "say that they'll locate a snake an' pile cactus around it an' make a corral so the rattler can't git out. I've never seen it myself."

"What's that?" Dan Shea demanded suddenly.

Off to the left there was motion. A mounted man appeared, small against the sky line, his horse running full out. As always, Dan Shea was impressed with distance. The mounted man was a bobbing doll, and the running horse seemed barely to move against the expanse of space, yet Dan Shea knew that the horse was swift and that it was the distance that lent the seeming slowness. The driver pulled his team to a halt.

"That's the duke," he said. "We'll wait a minute. He's headed this way. Mebbe we'll see somethin'."

"The duke?" Dan echoed.

"Name's Perrier. We call him the duke. He's an Englishman."

"What . . . ?" Dan began and stopped. Horse and rider were coming on, turned now so that their course would intersect the road. They grew in size rapidly. Before the team, two hundred yards away, a running wolf broke into the road, body low, tail carried between flying legs. The wolf disappeared and, almost instantly, his place was filled. There were four dogs that followed the wolf, great shaggy creatures running silently as the wolf had run, their heads flung forward, so intent on their quarry that they did not see the horses or the wagon. The dogs, too, disappeared into the brush, crowned out of it over a ridge in the sand and were gone.

"Here he comes!" There was excitement in the driver's voice.

Now on the road were the horse and rider. Dan had a glimpse, photographic in its clearness, of a small man, bolt upright in a saddle, of a magnificent horse that cleared the road at a leap, the rider seemingly a part of the mount. For an instant horse and man were framed in the road, and then they, too, were gone into the brush and over the ridge. The driver gathered up his lines. "He'll get that wolf too," the driver assured.

"But what . . . ?" Dan questioned.

"That's what he does," the driver explained. "The duke ain't got any particular place to stay. He's got a wagon an' a camp outfit an' he moves around with his dogs. He's got four of 'em, an' some of the best horses in the world, I guess. He's kind of crazy. The ranchmen pay him a bounty on the wolves he gets. Pretty near every time you see him he's ridin' with his dogs. Geddup! You, Buck, geddup!"

"He just hunts wolves?" Dan asked.

"Wolves an' coyotes. Won't shoot 'em. He hunts

'em horseback. Ever so often he comes into town. I guess he gets some money from the old country. Anyhow, that's what folks say."

"Oh." The situation was clear to Dan Shea now. Here and there in his travels he had met men who "got money from the old country." Most of them were no good. Dan Shea, having met them, could readily understand why they had been sent away. Of course there were exceptions, but . . .

Again the driver seemed to read Dan's thoughts. "The duke's all right," he said. "He's high an' mighty an' he don't talk much, but he's O.K." Having made that statement, the driver again lapsed into taciturnity.

The road went on. As it climbed toward the hills the country improved. The sand and rock, the desert growth, were left behind and grass supplanted them. Dan saw sheep, the herder sitting on a hillside, apparently asleep. The sheep were in good flesh and, to Dan Shea's expert eyes, of good breeding as well. The mountains approached and the sun was lower in the sky. Then again the greening tops of trees came into view, the road mounted a rise, turned and began a descent, then before the wagon a settlement appeared.

"El Puerto del Sol," the driver announced. "That's the big house up on the hill. That's where you'll go."

"Isn't there a hotel?" Dan asked. "Can't I get a place to stop?"

"Everybody goes to Don Martin's," the driver answered. "There ain't no hotel or nothin' else. Don Martin owns it all. Whoa, Buck. Whoa!" The wagon drew to a halt.

There were adobes clustered about, small houses

that settled, familiar and friendly, against the earth from which they had been made. A bright-eyed boy came running from the nearest dwelling and a man, gray-grizzled, walked out from a door and approached the wagon. The driver greeted the oldster.

"Buenas tardes, Jesus."

"Buenas tardes," Jesus answered. Dan Shea climbed down from the wagon seat. The driver spoke fluently, explaining that Dan Shea had come from Bendición.

"Eusabio," Jesus called. "Ven acá."

The boy answered, joining the three men. To him Jesus spoke again, directing that Dan Shea be taken to the hacienda. Dan Shea lifted his grip and rifle from the back of the wagon. The boy took them from his hands, his eyes bright as he handled the rifle, and said: "Come, señor" and led the way toward an opening between the buildings.

"You'll be all right," the driver assured. "Don Martin will look after you, Mr Shea. If you want to go back tomorrow I'll be leavin' about noon."

"Thanks," Dan answered and followed his guide.

Don Martin's hacienda was on the low rise above the clustered adobes. It was built square, around a patio, and there was a low and long portal across its front. At the entrance the boy Eusabio set down Dan's grip and lifted a heavy iron knocker, letting it fall to echo resoundingly. Within moments there was a shuffle of footsteps and an old man appeared. He smiled benignly at Dan, listened casually to Eusabio's explanation and, picking up the grip and gun, led the way into the patio. Dan followed. Seemingly at random, his guide selected a door, opened it and gestured to Dan to enter. The guide placed the grip inside the door, leaned the rifle against the jamb, smiled again and announced that Don Martin was with the sheep and that *el Señor* had but to call if he wished anything for his comfort. With that the old man shuffled away and Dan Shea, taking off his coat, set about removing some of the stains of travel. When he had finished he resumed the coat and went out into the patio.

Sundown had come. There was a mockingbird in the cottonwood tree that grew in the center of the patio. Dan Shea, seating himself on a bench, looked up at the bird and listened. The patio was cool and calm, and the bird's notes were liquid and softly sweet. When the mocker ceased his music Dan Shea pursed his lips and whistled, and in the tree the bird cocked his head to listen. From behind Dan a voice said: "He does not know that song. Listen." The words were followed by the liquid whistle of a scaled quail. In the tree the mocker half spread his wings, lowered them and hopped along his branch.

Again the quail whistled, and now the bird in the tree answered.

Dan Shea turned. There was a girl standing just under the shadow of the gallery behind him. He could see her face in the dusk, could see her dark eyes, the wealth of red-gold hair that made a misty halo about her head. She was tall for a woman, with wide full lips and high cheekbones. Her skin was gold, whether from the sun or from the rich blood that coursed beneath it, Dan could not tell. Altogether beautiful, altogether desirable, she stood there in her young womanhood, and Dan Shea caught his breath and felt his heart pound.

"You see?" the girl asked. "He knows that song."

Up in the tree the mocker whistled the quail call again.

Dan got up from the bench. Turning, he bowed to the girl. "I am Dan Shea," he said. "I've come to see Don Martin O'Connor."

The girl curtsied prettily. "I am Marillita O'Connor," she answered. "I make you welcome, señor."

There was a moment of awkward silence. How, Dan wondered, does one address divinity? From the front of the house there came noises, the tramp of feet, the sounds of a gruff voice speaking in Spanish. The door to the patio opened, and a giant of a man stood framed in the opening. Marillita ran toward the giant, and his arms swept her from her feet. Dan Shea stood watching.

The big man placed the girl on the ground and, holding her hand, came forward. Dan could see the resemblance now: the gray hair still tinged with its ruddy youth, the bold line of nose and face that in the girl was softened. He advanced a step. "Don Martin O'Connor?" he asked.

"The same," the giant rumbled.

"I am Dan Shea."

A smile broke across the crags of the man's face. "Shea, is it?" he demanded. "Irish by the look and name of you."

"My father came from Limerick," Dan Shea said.

Martin O'Connor's great hand engulfed Dan's, closing down until all the blood was drained from the fingers.

"A Limerick man and named Shea! Mary, here's a rare one. Come now, Mr Shea. This is my daughter Marillita, and what have you to say to that?"

Dan bowed again. There was nothing that he

could say. The girl's laughter rippled, and Dan Shea flushed.

"Hmmm," Martin O'Connor said dryly. "Ye've met then. What good luck brings you to us, Mr Shea?"

"I wanted to see you on a business matter."

O'Connor shook his head. "It's always business," he complained. "After supper we'll attend to it. Mary, keep the young man company while I set myself to rights. We're lambin', Mr Shea, an' it's a tryin', dirtyin' job, it is." With that he nodded to Dan and walked across the patio, entering a door on the farther side. Marillita O'Connor seated herself upon the bench and smiled up at Dan Shea.

"How does a girl go about keeping a young man company?" she asked archly.

Dan Shea sat down. "She sits and looks beautiful," he answered, smiling.

"Then I'm afraid I can't obey my father. I can sit . . ."

"And to look beautiful is something you can't help," Dan interrupted.

"Is the Blarney stone in Limerick, Mr Shea?"

"I've never seen the Blarney stone nor Limerick either. It's just the truth I speak."

The girl's laughter rilled like sparkling water. "Now I know you've seen them both," she declared. "You've kissed the Blarney stone too."

"No Blarney's needed here." Dan's eyes sparkled. "I'm as truthful as I would be on a witness stand."

When Don Martin returned he found his daughter and his guest sitting on either end of the bench, their eyes bright and laughter on their lips. Before he joined them Don Martin paused a moment on the gallery, smiling at the scene.

Supper was a leisurely meal eaten overlooking the patio. There were servants, deft and soft footed, to attend them, and the talk was of Ireland. O'Connor harked back into his memories, and the girl and the young man listened. Then when the meal was done and a lamp had been brought and placed on the table, O'Connor leaned back in his big chair and stared shrewdly at Dan Shea.

"You mentioned a matter of business," he prompted.

"I did, sir," Dan answered. "I've come down from Colorado and I've a plan that will make some money."

"Get on with it." O'Connor's voice was gruff.

"There are settlers coming into the San Luis Valley," Dan Shea said. "All of southern Colorado is being settled. It's a sheep country and they need sheep. I plan to supply them."

"So?" The don's great bushy eyebrows lifted. "It's a sheepman you are then?"

"I know sheep," Dan answered briefly. "I plan to get sheep in the New Mexico Territory and drive them north. The market's good and there's money in the scheme."

"And you want to buy sheep from me?"

Dan moved his hands in a little negative gesture. "I've no money to buy sheep," he said frankly. "The panic wiped me out. I want a partner in the business."

"Me, for instance?"

"It looks foolish for me to talk this way, Don Martin." Dan Shea was very earnest. "But I've friends in Denver, people that no doubt you know. You could write them concerning me."

Martin O'Connor shook his great white head. "I make up my own mind about a man," he proclaimed. "I'll not need to write or ask. I'll need to see. The plan sounds fine, indeed it does." He paused, and Dan's hopes rose high. "Except that I've no need of money," O'Connor concluded.

"Then you aren't interested?"

A sly smile twitched at O'Connor's lips beneath his mustache. "I didn't say that," he demurred. "You'll stay a day or two, Mr Shea, an' we'll talk it over."

Dan nodded.

Don Martin arose ponderously. "Come with me in the mornin', Mr Shea," he invited. "I'll be busy, but we'll have a chance to talk. You've been given a bed?"

"Yes sir." Dan, too, was on his feet.

"The day starts early," O'Connor warned. "I'm for bed. Come, Mary."

Marillita O'Connor flashed a smile at Dan Shea and then, tucking her hand beneath her father's arm, accompanied him. Dan watched them go into the darkness out of the lamplight.

CHAPTER FOUR:

"LOUSY SHEEPMAN"

In the morning, with all El Puerto del Sol stirring about him, Dan Shea joined Martin O'Connor at breakfast. Marillita did not appear, and the two men ate alone and in silence. After the meal they left the house. A buckboard was ready in front of the barn, and Dan climbed into the seat beside his host. Don Martin drove the buckboard toward the east, squarely into the rising sun. Within half an hour after leaving the hacienda they were among the sheep.

The lambing grounds were long hill slopes, warm in the sun and with green grass filling the little draws between them. There were herders with the flocks, and the black coals of fires showed that men had been on duty through the night. Their camps were adjacent to the lambing grounds, and in those camps men slept.

At each stopping place Don Martin was greeted. There was something of awe, something of respect and something more of love in the greetings. It was as though Don Martin O'Connor were a feudal lord, a great and well-beloved *patrón*, and these his serfs. The don asked questions and received answers. He gave directions and received cheerful assurances of obedience. Dan Shea listened. Once he asked a question of his own, and when the buckboard rolled on Don Martin looked at him and asked sharply: "You've the Spanish?"

"I've learned it," Dan Shea answered.

At ten o'clock they were well north and east of the hacienda, and here they stopped. There was a large band of ewes, and with the sheep was but one man and a small boy. Don Martin alighted and went to the sheep. When he came back he was scowling. "Trouble here," he said briefly. "A rascal of a herder ran away and another's sick. I'll have to help." He reached into the bed of the buckboard as he spoke and pulled out a pair of heavy duck overalls.

Dan Shea got down from the seat. "Have you another pair?" he asked.

A flash of astonishment showed briefly on O'Connor's face and then was gone. "I might find you a pair," he answered and reached into the buckboard again. Dan Shea, going to the front of the buckboard, leaned forward and unhooked the tugs. When O'Connor came around the team, carrying another pair of overalls, Dan was freeing the neck-yoke and lowering the tongue to the ground.

They tied the team to the wheels of the buckboard. O'Connor sent the boy scurrying over the hill on an errand, and then both men fell to work.

Ewes are not good mothers. When a lamb is born it is necessary to make the ewe claim it. If ever mother and lamb are separated there is trouble. So at lambing time sheepmen stay with their flocks, keeping each ewe and newborn lamb segregated so that the ewe will claim her own. After a time, after the lamb has nursed, after the ewe has been forced to furnish food from her maternal fount, the trouble usually ends. But if the grass is short and the ewe has no milk for her lamb, if they become separated, if any one of a hundred things happens, then there is an orphan and a ewe that has milk but no lamb to take it.

Martin O'Connor and Dan Shea fell to work. Lambs had been born during the night, and of these some had been definitely deserted. It was necessary that the lambs and ewes be paired, that the ewes be made to let the lambs nurse, that families, even though they were not mother and offspring, be formed. It was a trying, wearisome, annoying task, but it had to be done. Dan Shea knew how and so did Martin O'Connor and the pastor with the flock. They attacked the job systematically and obstinately. Now and then Martin O'Connor looked up from his own work, across the woolly backs and greening grass to where Dan Shea labored and, after each inspection, he chuckled.

The boy came back across the hill bringing three men. These, after a word with Don Martin, fell to work, and O'Connor, leaving them, came to Dan Shea.

Dan was skinning a dead lamb. Beyond him was a ewe, her udder showing that she had a lamb, but the lamb was not in evidence. Dan, as he skinned the lamb, kept another little fellow pinned to the earth beneath his leg. He looked up briefly as O'Connor arrived.

"This is her lamb," Dan said, indicating the dead animal with his knife. "She won't take the other."

O'Connor grunted. Dan finished flaying off the pelt, placed the pelt upon the back of the live lamb and tied it there with the dangling strings of hide that had been legs. He released the lamb, and it wabbled unsteadily toward the ewe who repulsed it. Dan caught the ewe and held her despite her struggles. When she quieted the lamb butted his head into her flank and found a teat. The ewe turned her head, nosed the lamb, smelling it, and, apparently either accepting the lamb as her own or acknowledging the inevitable, was quiet. Dan held her awhile longer and then released her. She did not drive the lamb away, and Dan turned to Don Martin. Martin O'Connor was smiling slyly.

"We can go on now," he said.

Stripped of the duck overalls, back on the comfortable seat of the buckboard, with the country flying by under the rolling wheels, Don Martin made explanation.

"I've eighty thousand sheep," he said abruptly. "About that many, anyhow. Some of them I run myself."

Dan nodded.

"The other sheep," Don Martin continued, watching the backs of the trotting horses, "I put out on shares." He glanced briefly at Dan. "I take a *partidario*," the don continued. "I make an agreement with him. I give him so many sheep: so many ewes, so many wethers, so many bucks. I get two pounds of wool a head when we shear and twenty per cent of the lambs. At the end of five years my *partidario* pays me back the sheep I gave him."

Dan nodded.

"They live and I live," Don Martin amplified. "I look after them. Is there anything wrong with that?"

Dan shook his head.

"Those were my sheep you helped with back

there," O'Connor disclosed. "I'm lookin' for a *partidario* at that place. There's a good house and grass and water. It will handle ten thousand head of sheep." He eyed Dan narrowly.

"A good thing for someone," Dan agreed.

"A man might make some money," O'Connor continued.

"About what do the sheep shear?" Dan asked.

O'Connor pursed his lips. "Four or five pounds, maybe," he answered. "I've been using heavy shearing bucks. We'll look at some bucks when we get back."

"You sell the wool in the East?"

"I do. I've been selling lambs in California, too, but they've sheep of their own out there now. The market's dropped."

"In Colorado . . ." Dan began.

"We'll talk tonight," O'Connor interrupted. "There's the house that I spoke of. It's a good house."

Dan looked at the square rock building. He saw the sheds and corrals behind it, saw the little stream that came trickling down from the hills to furnish water.

"A good place," he agreed.

Don Martin turned the buckboard, and they headed back toward the southeast.

All the way back conversation was lacking between the two. Martin O'Connor was engaged in thought, and Dan respected his companion's preoccupation. When they reached the hacienda the don turned the team over to a man at the barn and led the way to the big house. In the patio the two men separated, each going to his room. Dan cleaned up, put on a fresh shirt taken from his grip and wiped the dust from his boots. Returning to the patio, he found Marillita.

The two talked for a time, Marillita asking questions concerning Denver and the country to the north, and Dan answering them. The table was laid on the gallery. Martin O'Connor joined his daughter and guest, and the three sat down.

When the meal was finished Don Martin brought out cigars, passed one to Dan Shea and nodded to his daughter. "I'll talk some business with Mr Shea," he said briefly. The girl made a small grimace of distaste but got up, smiled at Dan and went into the house. O'Connor leaned back in his chair and puffed smoke toward the porch roof.

"I'm sixty years old," he announced. "Forty years ago I came here without a cent in my pockets, as green a lad as ever sailed from Ireland."

Dan made no comment. None was necessary or expected.

"I came to Santa Fe with a wagon train," O'Connor continued. "From there I came on down here and here I stayed. I married Marillita's mother. In time she inherited El Puerto del Sol. I've built it since then. Built it with sheep."

Dan nodded. The night was growing all about, and the lamp glowed yellow on the table.

"It's Marillita's when I'm gone," Martin O'Connor supplemented, looking narrowly at Dan Shea.

"A big place," Dan commented.

O'Connor took the cigar from his mouth and looked at it. "How did you happen to come West?" he asked suddenly.

Dan shrugged. "I was in the war," he answered. "When it was over I didn't go back. My people were dead and there was nothing to take me home. I came West and worked in the mines around Cripple Creek. Mining didn't suit. I worked for a buffalo hunter awhile and then took out my own outfit. The buffalo are playing out. I bought wagons and horses and went to freighting. I got too big for my own good. The panic wiped me out. I paid my debts and started over."

"You know sheep," O'Connor reminded.

"We raised them before the war," Dan explained.

O'Connor said, "Hmmm," and returned the cigar to his mouth. Smoke trailed up in the lamplight. "I've got to get a man for Rancho Norte," he commented.

Dan stared moodily at the lamp. He was thinking of the years behind him, recollection stirred in his mind by O'Connor's question. Martin O'Connor puffed the cigar to life, removed it from his lips and spoke again.

"I'll not let you have the sheep to drive to Colorado," he announced brusquely. "Maybe there's money to be made there; maybe not. If it's a good idea somebody else will try it. I'll wait an' see how they come out."

Dan was silent for a moment. Then: "I don't blame you," he said. "They're your sheep, and I told you I had no money to buy them. But the first man to drive to that market will get the cream."

O'Connor's eyes were narrow as he watched his guest. "The cream from sheep comes in raisin' 'em," he said. "Well, good night."

"Good night."

"Take the lamp with you."

"Thanks."

Martin O'Connor hoisted himself to his feet and paused. "Tomorrow," he said, "I'll be goin' in to Bendición. I've a man in mind for Rancho Norte an' I want to get him. Likely you'll ride with me? The mail wagon doesn't go to town tomorrow."

"I'll be obliged for the ride," Dan Shea said.

"Good night then." O'Connor's voice was curt.

The following morning Dan Shea packed his grip. Again he and his host occupied the breakfast table without company. Again they went out to the barn and found the buckboard waiting. Marillita had not appeared. Dan had searched the empty patio with his eyes and had seen no sign of the girl. He put his grip and rifle into the buckboard while Don Martin mounted to the seat. Dan stood beside a wheel. "I'd like to say good-by and thank Miss O'Connor for her hospitality," he announced.

"She'll not be up yet," O'Connor answered briefly. "Get in, Shea. I'll give her your thanks."

Dan climbed into the buckboard.

Don Martin drove a team as though they were made of iron and not of flesh and blood. He kept the horses at a steady trot, covering country, putting the distance behind him. They lost sight of El Puerto del Sol after the first rise was crossed. They dropped down across the grassland and sighted the thin line of trees that marked Alamo Creek. Dan made comment as they reached the stream. "Coming out," he said, "I saw a man chasing a wolf with dogs. The mail driver said that his name was Perrier."

"I've paid him bounty on many a pelt," Don Martin said. "The duke, they call him."

"That's a queer way to make a living."

"He does it for sport!" O'Connor's words were curt. He did not look at Dan Shea but continued to watch the horses and the road. It was evident that Martin O'Connor did not want to talk. Dan let the silence take them.

Reaching Bendición, they found the little town was busy as an anthill. The hitch rails around the plaza were crowded with saddle horses and teams. There were men on the sidewalks, men and women in the stores. On the grass of the plaza little knots of people were congregated, here a group of dark-skinned natives, here burly men from the mines. Lanky riders leaned against the sides of buildings; saloon doors banged open and banged shut; from the stores came clerks and patrons carrying purchases to waiting wagons. Don Martin O'Connor stopped his buckboard before the hotel, and Dan Shea climbed out.

"Thanks for the ride and for your hospitality," he said, lifting his belongings from the back of the buckboard. "You'll tell Miss O'Connor that I'm sorry I didn't get to say good-by?"

"I'll do that." Don Martin was gruff. "You'll be welcome if you come to El Puerto del Sol again."

"I hope to," Dan answered. "Thanks again. Good-by."

"Adiós." The buckboard turned with a scrape of cramped wheels, and Martin O'Connor sent his team along the side of the plaza. Dan, his grip dangling, entered the hotel and, dropping the grip beside the desk, asked for a room.

The clerk accepted the payment for the room and gave Dan a key. When Dan commented on Bendición's activity the clerk shrugged. This, the clerk said, was Saturday and the first of the month. The mines had paid off and the miners were in town. There were many people, the clerk said, who came in from the surrounding territory to buy and to spend. Dan nodded, replaced the key on the desk and went out on the street again.

There was disappointment in Dan Shea. He had entertained high hopes of interesting Martin O'Connor in his idea. Those hopes were gone glimmering, and he must start over. As he walked down the street away from the hotel, Dan planned his next move. He turned the corner at the east end of the plaza and paused. There was a group of men across from him. Separated from this group, perhaps ten feet intervening, George Delaney stood talking with a heavy-bodied bearded man. Dan saw Delaney and turned his head away. Anger rose in Dan at the sight of Delaney. Some inner urge prompted Dan to look back again, and he saw that the young lawyer was watching him. The bearded man turned his head, cast a hasty glance at Dan and then moved so that his back was toward the sidewalk.

Dan was startled. Somewhere within the last few days he had seen that bearded face. He was certain of it! Delaney talked to his companion, now and again lifting his eyes so that he looked at Dan Shea. Dan walked on, his anger somewhat dulled by his curiosity. He reached Fitzpatrick's saloon, went in and found Fitzpatrick behind the bar.

The two men shook hands. "What luck?" Fitzpatrick asked.

"No luck at all." Dan shook his head. "I talked with O'Connor. He won't let me have any sheep."

"I've been askin' some questions," Fitzpatrick

volunteered. "Ramon de la Luz is sore because you jumped his friend Delaney. You can't get any of Ramon's sheep, but there's a place west of here that might be just the ticket."

"Whereabouts?" Dan asked.

"Over by Rio Salado. I'll find out a little more an' let you know."

Dan nodded. Fitzpatrick's friendship was good after his disappointment.

"Youtsey," Fitzpatrick said, changing the subject abruptly, "has been round again askin' about the murder. He wanted to know where you were, an' I told him. Youtsey don't like me much an' he figures you're a friend of mine. He . . ."

"Fitz!" Dan's interruption was sharp. "That's it!"

"What's it?" Fitzpatrick's voice showed his surprise.

"The man with Delaney!" Dan caught Fitzpatrick's arm and urged him toward the door. "He was one of those men at the stage station!"

"What?"

"On the corner." They were at the door now, and Dan was looking out toward the corner. "He was standing there talking to Delaney. One of the men that killed Maples. I know it was."

"Where is he?" Fitzpatrick demanded.

Dan shook his head. "He's gone now. So is Delaney. They were standing there talking when I came in."

Fitzpatrick stepped out the door, Dan beside him. "See him anyplace?" Fitzpatrick asked.

"I don't see him now," Dan admitted. "But he was there just a minute ago."

"Did he see you?" Fitzpatrick asked.

"Yes."

The saloonkeeper grunted. "He's pulled out then," he said.

"I'm going around the square," Dan announced. "Maybe I'll see him." Without waiting for Fitzpatrick's answer he swung away. Fitzpatrick remained in the doorway, examining the square with his eyes.

Dan made the circuit of the plaza. He looked into the stores, entered the saloons, examined the men he met and passed. He did not see Delaney or the man who had been with him. Dan was back at the corner, close to Fitzpatrick's saloon, before he paused. Fitzpatrick still stood in the doorway looking toward Dan. Dan shook his head as a sign to his friend that the search had been fruitless. There was a little group crossing from the plaza toward the corner: three men. Dan stepped down into the street and started to cross.

In the center of the street he met the three from the plaza and shifted to give them passage. They were cowmen, booted, spurred, hats pushed back, faces flushed, more than a little drunk. As Dan moved so, too, did the three, blocking his way. Dan recognized the men who had been in Fitzpatrick's saloon the night of his arrival at Bendición. One of the three, the youngest, stopped, confronting Dan Shea.

"Git out of the way, sheepherder," the cowboy rasped.

Anger, quick and hot, arose in Dan. He did not move.

"I said git out of the way," the puncher growled. "You Goddamned sheepherders think you own the street."

"Tell him, Buster." One of the group urged the youngster on. "Make the bastard move."

Around Dan's mouth the muscles tightened. His eyes were bleak. Dan Shea said nothing.

Buster, emboldened by Dan's silence and his companion's encouragement, reached out a hand and pushed against Dan's chest. Dan took a single step back.

"He don't want a fight," Buster's friend crowed. "Look at the sonofabitch back up. Lousy sheepherder. He . . ."

It was too much. Dan Shea's quiet broke into swift, devastating action. Buster, he slapped with his open hand. Taking the blow squarely on his cheek, Buster reeled, his hat flying. Dan Shea, all repression forgotten and lost, closed in. His fists were swift as striking snakes and as devastating as ax blows. Buster sat down in the street, his eyes vacant, one hand mechanically feeling his jaw. The other man went staggering back.

Fists were new to these riders. They were strong enough and they did not lack courage and willingness, but they were no match for Dan Shea. The third man, dodging a blow, stumbled into another and dropped across the sitting Buster's legs, to remain there.

The man who had backed before Dan's swift attack was reaching for his gun. Fitzpatrick, running from his doorway, had reached the scene. He stopped the reaching hand. "Hold it!" Fitzpatrick warned. His voice was sharp, but that alone did not check the movement. Rather the fact that Fitzpatrick himself held a weapon deterred the puncher.

Dan Shea, head lowered belligerently, blue eyes hot beneath his black brows, stood poised, and from the stores, from the street, from the plaza, men came to form a crowd, pushing in all about.

"That's the boy," Fitzpatrick praised as the third cowpuncher brought his hand away empty from his hip. "That's the boy!"

Youtsey, face red with exertion, breath short from running, pushed through the crowd and faced Dan Shea. "What's this?" the sheriff demanded. "What's goin' on here? Shea, you're disturbin' the peace. You're under arrest."

Anger still possessed Dan Shea. He looked at the sheriff, and under the glare of his eyes Youtsey recoiled.

"You couldn't arrest one side of me," Dan told Youtsey. "Try it!"

"By glory . . ." Youtsey began.

"It was them that started it, Sheriff." Fitzpatrick spoke placatingly. "They were drunk. Nobody's hurt."

That was true. Buster had regained his feet. His hat was in his hand, placed there by some bystander, and he stared at it foolishly. His companion had risen from the street and, eyes still bewildered, was staring at Buster. The man Fitzpatrick had discouraged was gone, merging with the crowd.

"Three of 'em," a voice said. "Did you see it start, Fred? He knocked two down just like that."

"It was them that started it, Sheriff," Fitzpatrick repeated earnestly.

Youtsey stood undecided, glaring at Dan. "You can't pull a thing like this in my town," he declared hotly. "Shea, I'll . . ."

"What's the trouble here?" a voice boomed. Men moved away. Through the lane that had opened for him Don Martin O'Connor moved majestically.

"What's the trouble?" he repeated as he stopped. "Mr Shea's a friend of mine, Sheriff. I hope nothin's happened to him."

The belligerence faded from Youtsey's face as he looked at Martin O'Connor. His voice was obsequious. "Some drunks tried to jump Mr Shea. I was just goin' to arrest 'em. You want to make a complaint, Mr Shea?"

Dan shook his head. He was staring unbelievingly at Youtsey. Youtsey, flushing under the stare, turned back to the onlookers. "Go on now," he ordered sharply. "Nothin' to stand around here for. Go on now!"

Martin O'Connor slipped his hand familiarly under Dan's arm. "I was just going to hunt you up," he announced. The hand urged Dan forward. Fitzpatrick, a smile glinting in his eyes, fell in place on Dan's right. Again a way opened, and the three passed through.

They went to Fitzpatrick's saloon. There, in the coolness of the barroom, away from all the crowd, they stopped. O'Connor, releasing Dan's arm, boomed his laughter.

"What started it?" he demanded, the laughter done, but a chuckle still in his voice. "I didn't see the whole thing. I'm too old to run like a boy. What happened, Shea?"

"They were drunk," Dan said curtly. "I lost my temper."

Fitzpatrick's drawl was dryly humorous. "I'd say you mislaid it, anyhow. They called him a lousy sheepman an' he didn't like it."

Don Martin's eyes narrowed. "Ain't you a sheepman?" he demanded.

"I'll take what they said from nobody!" Dan's

temper was beginning to rise again. "I'm obliged to you, Don Martin. The sheriff was going to try to arrest me until you came along. I'm grateful. I . . ."

"Now wait a minute," Martin O'Connor interrupted, the twinkle growing in his eyes. "Ain't you a sheepman?"

"I haven't any sheep," Dan Shea said. "They started to curse me and I wouldn't stand for it. That's all. I'm obliged to you, but . . ."

"An' whose fault is it that you've no sheep?" There was a note of asperity in O'Connor's voice. "Your wits aren't as quick as your fists, Shea. Here I am with nobody at Rancho Norte, an' you with no sheep. Now what do you think of that?"

"But you said you were coming to town to see a man," Dan reminded. "You said you had a man in mind for the place."

"An' I had," O'Connor agreed. "There was an Irish lad I had in mind. I hinted an' talked, an' the thickhead wouldn't say a word."

"You mean . . . ?" Light began to dawn on Dan Shea. "Would you take me for a *partidario* on Rancho Norte, Don Martin? Would you?"

Don Martin O'Connor's great hand descended between Dan Shea's shoulders, almost driving his breath away. "An' who else?" O'Connor boomed. "Who else did you think I had in mind? Of all the dumb ones! An' Irish too!"

"Then . . ." Dan Shea began and caught his breath. "Then you'll . . ."

"From now on, Mr Shea," Don Martin O'Connor interrupted gravely, "they'll be speakin' the truth when they call you a sheepman. You can still resint the 'lousy.'" His great hand shoved against Dan

Shea's back, and his laughter boomed. "We'll take a drink on it," he completed when his glee was satisfied. "You an' your friend. Come on now." Again his great laugh rang out.

CHAPTER FIVE:
MASTER OF THE HUNT

El Puerto del Sol engulfed Dan Shea. Like some insatiable monster it took him into its maw. His energy became fuel for El Puerto del Sol, his intelligence a part of its intelligence. His labor, his sweat, his thought, his very being belonged to the grant. And as young Dan Shea became a part of El Puerto del Sol, so, too, El Puerto entered into his blood and became a part of him.

Martin O'Connor wasted no time in using his new *partidario*. Dan Shea, installed at Rancho Norte, sleeping in a tent among the cottonwoods along the creek—Hilario Bargas, his wife Domisinda and their numerous brood living in the rock house and caring for the new *patrón*—went immediately to work. The lambing was still in progress, and Dan plunged into it, a new broom sweeping clean, a fresh strong tide in the affairs of the ranch.

With the lambing finished other work pressed. As a *partidario*, Dan Shea had sheep to receive. So now Martin O'Connor and his *mayordomo*, Salvador Ocano, grizzled and sharp faced, came to Rancho Norte, and following them came Dan's sheep. There was dust in the corrals, and ewes blatted and lambs used their small high voices. Sheep were mouthed and counted and marked and released in the care of herders who worked for the new *partidario*. The work was endless and the sun was high and hot. And then suddenly that seemingly endless work was done and Dan Shea stood beside Martin O'Connor and watched the last of his sheep go trailing out toward the east and the good grass along the Packsaddles.

"Now," Martin O'Connor announced, "we'll take a rest, the two of us."

Dan stared at the departing sheep, then he looked at the big man beside him. "I'd like to know why you did this for me, Don Martin," Dan said slowly.

O'Connor stared out across the barren earth toward the creek and the cottonwoods. "You're Irish," he answered shortly. "So am I."

Dan waited. Presently O'Connor continued, his voice slow, as though he were finding the words somewhere in his mind. "You're honest an' you'll fight. That much I know. Someday I'll be gone and Marillita will have El Puerto del Sol. O'Connors ain't liked in this country, Dan." His blue eyes, frank and open, searched Dan's face.

A long silence held between them, both men thinking of the words that had been spoken. Then Dan Shea made his answer, vowing his fealty and binding himself, voicing the grip that El Puerto del Sol had upon him and he upon El Puerto del Sol.

"She'll have one."

That was all he said. It was enough. All the strength of Dan Shea, all his skill, all his wisdom, was promised in those words. And Martin O'Connor, looking at the man who stood beside him, was satisfied. Here was the man he wanted, the man in whose hands he could place all this vast domain that he had erected and fought for and for which he would die. There was no doubting Dan Shea. He stood sturdy and foursquare, facing the future: his future and that of El Puerto del Sol.

"It's a sudden country," Martin O'Connor said. "Things happen quick sometimes. Come now, Dan. We'll go to the hacienda. Marillita will be expectin' us. You've neglected her these past weeks. Come now."

And so at Don Martin's behest Dan went to the hacienda. He made himself as presentable as possible before he left Rancho Norte, but for all that he was a wild enough figure when he stopped his horse beside Don Martin's stables. Hair long and beard curling blackly on his face, clothing clean enough but rough, hat a battered pancake atop his head, rifle in his saddle boot, Dan Shea was as typical of the time and place as was the great house itself. Marillita saw him so and smiled and, not waiting for his coming, went to her room.

Before the evening meal Don Martin's servant trimmed Dan's beard and hair. His boots were greased with tallow and his clothing set to rights so that when he appeared in the patio some of the roughness was lost. Martin O'Connor nodded approvingly at Dan's appearance, and when his daughter came to join them O'Connor's eyes crinkled at the corners as he smiled, albeit he said not a word. The girl was dressed in her best, in clothing that had come across the continent by railroad and wagon train, and she was beautiful as sunrise. Her hair, its redness gleaming with gold, was ordered carefully; her dress emphasized rather than concealed, and her smile when she greeted Dan Shea was the smile of a great lady condescending to a subject. Dan was properly impressed and throughout the meal spoke very seldom and ate but little, keeping his eyes on the girl.

That night, pleading fatigue, Martin O'Connor went early to his room and, with his light extinguished, sat beside his window and listened to the voices in the patio, Dan's deep, masculine rumble and the lighter tones of Marillita. Occasionally O'Connor smiled.

For two days Dan Shea stayed at the hacienda of El Puerto del Sol. On the morning of the third day he bade his host and hostess good-by and rode back to Rancho Norte.

The rock house was deserted when he arrived. Hilario was not at the corrals nor was Domisinda in the kitchen. Even the children were gone. Dan walked all around the house and to his own bedroom beside the creek and found no one. But there were voices coming from a grove of trees further along the stream, and when he reached the grove he found his absent ones. There was a wagon amid the cottonwoods, and horses grazed there and, when Dan approached, a great dog, tall as a calf and heavy, barred his way silently, with fangs exposed. Dan regarded the dog and the wagon and the group about it and walked forward fearlessly. The dog gave way and Dan, stopping beside the group, spoke a greeting.

"Good day, sir."

Hilario fell back a step and then retreated ignominiously to the corrals. Domisinda, seeing her *patrón*, shrilled to her brood and scurried away toward the house and, from the wagon tongue where he had been seated, a small, sandy man arose and, taking his pipe from between his teeth, answered the salutation.

"Good day."

Dan stood, undergoing the inspection of shrewd blue eyes. When it was finished the small man advanced a step. "Mr Shea?" he said.

Dan nodded briefly.

"I am Esme Perrier." The small man's hand was outstretched. Dan took it.

"I've made myself at home here," Perrier announced.

"You're quite welcome," Dan said formally.

The dog that had met him pushed against his hand, lowering her head to do so.

"Mind your manners, Mab!" Perrier ordered.

Dan's hand fondled the dog's ears. At the end of the wagon there were others, great gaunt brutes, their muzzles grizzled, their bodies covered with coarse, straight hair.

"Why," said Dan Shea, "they're wolfhounds."

A twinkle came into Perrier's blue eyes. "Irish wolfhounds," he corrected. "Sit down, Mr Shea." His gesture as he indicated the wagon tongue was courtly.

Dan sat down. Mab, following him, crouched at his feet and looked up with liquid eyes. Automatically Dan's hand sought her head, working the silky ears. Perrier, legs widespread, arms crossed, pipe in hand, stood looking at his guest and the dog. He shook his head. "I've never seen Mab do that before," he said querulously. "Would you mind an experiment, Mr Shea?"

"No."

"Puck. Here!"

From the dogs at the wagon end one great fellow arose and, stately as royalty, came to his master. Perrier looked at Dan. "Call him," he directed.

"Puck, come here!" Dan ordered.

Without hesitation the great dog left Perrier and approached. He lowered his head, allowing Dan to scratch behind his ears and then, tongue lolling with evident enjoyment, stretched himself at Dan's feet.

Perrier puffed twice upon his pipe, removed it, looked at its brown bowl as though he had never seen the pipe before and spoke again. "I would not believe this unless I saw it," he stated.

"The dogs?" Dan questioned.

"The dogs. They'll go to no one but me."

Dan stroked Puck's head the while Mab looked on jealously. "I've a way with dogs," Dan said.

"It's evident." Perrier knocked out his pipe against the heel of his hand and seated himself. "You're new here, Mr Shea," he announced.

"Yes," Dan agreed. "I've taken Rancho Norte to run for Don Martin."

"You've no objection to my hunting?" Perrier asked.

"I'll be glad to have you hunt."

"Perhaps you'll join me?" The blue eyes were sharp.

"Thanks. I will."

Esme Perrier cocked one booted foot across the other, clasped his hands above his upraised knee and leaned back. "Perhaps you'll care for some explanations?" he asked.

"Not unless you choose." Dan was smiling.

"Why, then I'll choose." The blue eyes were bright and twinkling. "I've hounds here, and horses. I hunt wolves and coyotes. I'm master of the hunt. You understand, Mr Shea?"

"Yes." Dan smiled. "You hunt wolves and coyotes."

"You're Irish, Mr Shea?" Perrier's smile was easy as Dan's own.

"American. My father was a Limerick man."

Perrier clasped his hands together. From the end of the wagon, silent footed as a cloud, a man appeared. "Robert," Perrier announced, "Mr Shea will be my guest at dinner."

"Yes sir." Robert's sunburned face was blank.

"You'll stay?" Perrier eyed his guest.

"Thank you," Dan Shea responded.

"Wolves and coyotes," Perrier said. "They're quite different from the fox. You've hunted foxes, Mr Shea?"

"I've never had the pleasure."

"Ah well, you'll find this exciting enough. I've a horse that's up to your weight, I believe."

"I've horses," Dan Shea responded.

Perrier disregarded the statement. His eyes ran over Dan's long body. "Wellington will carry you nicely," he announced. "I'll expect you at seven, Mr Shea."

Dan recognized dismissal. He got up and nodded briefly. "At seven," he said. "Good-by, Mr Perrier."

Perrier made no answer. Dan touched each dog as they stood beside him, nodded again and walked out of the grove.

Back at the house Hilario and the details of Rancho Norte engulfed Dan Shea. Hilario had visited each band of sheep and now reported. Shea listened and asked questions, nodding approval at the answers. The details of his home-coming attended, Dan took Hilario with him to a spot some little distance from the house. Here he stopped and gestured. "I want to build a house here, Hilario," he announced. "A small house of rock. Can it be done?"

"¿Por qué no?" Hilario responded. "My cousin Anastacio is a rock mason. But why a house, Señor Dan?"

Dan Shea bent and picked up a stick. "Because I want it," he answered. "Here, Hilario. I want the house so." With Hilario following, Dan Shea drew a pattern on the dusty ground, a long wall, a shorter wall: three rooms in all.

Hilario bobbed his head. "*Si*," he approved. "*Si*, Señor Dan. *Mañana . . .*"

"Tomorrow then," Dan Shea said. "We'll get the rock from the hill."

Dan presented himself at the grove promptly at seven. There was a table laid close beside the wagon, and a fire burned in a pit behind it. With all the ceremony of a man welcoming another to his home, Perrier greeted his guest and led him to the table. They sat down together, and the silent Robert served them.

When the meal was done Robert brought wine, and Perrier, rising, lifted his glass. Dan Shea, too, arose.

"To a pleasant meeting," Perrier said, and they drank.

Dan Shea did not stay long following the meal. Perrier talked briefly of wolves and their habits, of horses, of dogs, of the country as seen from the viewpoint of a hunter. Dan listened, rarely adding a word. The lantern suspended above the table, burned yellow, and insects besieged it. At nine o'clock Dan bade his host good night, promising to be on hand early the following morning. Walking back to his camp beside the creek, he considered Perrier, his dwelling, his occupation and his reticence. Curiosity piqued Dan Shea. What was Perrier's background? The small, blue-eyed man and the immaculate, silent servant formed an enigma that Dan Shea could not penetrate or solve.

With the rising sun of a new day throwing light into his eyes, Dan got up and dressed. He ate breakfast hastily and then, saddling a horse at the barn, mounted and rode to the grove. Perrier, meeting him just at the edge of the trees, frowned and shook his head when he saw Dan's horse.

"He'll hardly carry you over rough country," Perrier announced. "No matter. I've a horse that will."

Dan dismounted and, leading his horse, followed the slight man. Perrier took him into the grove, stopped and, pointing to one of three horses that were tied side by side, said: "Take Wellington there. He's in need of riding."

Robert, booted, with a cap on his head, appeared on the scene. "Shall I change the saddle, sir?" he asked.

"Never mind," Dan ordered. "I'll attend to it."

Perrier stood by, smiling, while Dan Shea shifted his saddle from one horse to the other. When the girths were tight the small man said: "If you're ready?"

Leading Wellington, Dan followed Perrier.

Perrier's horse was a bay, a magnificent animal at least seventeen hands high and weighing perhaps twelve hundred pounds. The little man went up like a jockey, settled himself on the flat saddle and nodded to Dan. Dan, too, mounted, feeling the spring steel of his horse beneath him and, still with Perrier leading, they left the grove, the dogs following silently behind them.

They rode toward the east, Perrier restraining his horse, Dan feeling Wellington's pull against the bit. Once they were clear of the ranch Perrier occasionally rose in his stirrups to scan the country and, atop a ridge, they paused.

"They run by sight," Perrier said, speaking of the dogs. "I've often thought that foxhounds would be better but . . . Hullo! there's one!"

He pointed to the east. Below them in the valley, shielded from the sun, there was motion. Dan could see an animal, minute in the distance, moving along through the oak brush. Perrier swung his horse until his right side was toward the valley and called sharply: "Puck!"

The great dog came at command. Perrier thrust out his right stirrup and Puck, raising up, placed his feet upon his master's boot and gazed intently into the valley. Perrier continued to point. "There, Puck! There!"

Suddenly the dog dropped down. He bayed once, his voice a roar rather than the sound made by any ordinary dog, and then he was gone. The others followed Puck, sweeping silently away like a tidal wave. Perrier reined his horse around, glanced at Dan Shea on the back of the dancing Wellington and said: "Now!"

Dan gave rein. Instantly under him, with a grinding of hoofs against stone, Wellington bunched his mighty haunches. Down the hill they went.

It was like nothing Dan Shea had ever experienced. The great horse flew. Dan could ride; he could sit a saddle, but never before had he ridden such a horse. They came to oak and crashed through it. Wellington did not pause or hesitate. A ditch crossed the way. They were over it. Beyond the ditch the hillside arose, steep and brush covered. They went up the hill as though it did not exist. The wind streamed by, and the blood rushed in Dan Shea's veins, and all the wild thrill of the hunt filled him. Beside him Perrier was shouting, and Dan lifted his own voice in savage outcry, harking back across the years to the wild men who had run their game on horseback.

The hill accomplished, Dan went down the further slope. The dogs were closer now, running silently. Beyond the dogs a great lobo wolf ran, tail curled between his legs, looking back as he ran, fangs exposed. Puck and Mab were in the lead of the pack and Dan was almost on the heels of the rearmost dog.

The wolf dodged, turning swiftly. The dogs ran past, pell-mell, trying to turn. Dan brought his horse around, reining sharply to the right. Mab and Puck had not been fooled by the dodging. They were separated now, knowing that the end was nearly come. Puck followed the wolf while Mab cut across the circle. Dan Shea followed Mab. There, where tangent and arc met, Mab sprang in. Big as the wolf, as well armed, dog and lobo were evenly matched. Dan reined Wellington to a halt. Puck came leaping. The lobo, gallant at his death, met the two fairly but was no match for them. There was a tangle of flying bodies, a snarling, and then the wolf was stretched out and the dogs were worrying him. Dan swung down from his horse and strode forward. "Puck!" he commanded. "Down, boy!" The other dogs came piling in.

Rock flew and clattered. Perrier, dropping down, stepped forward with his riding crop. The dogs ceased worrying the dead wolf and slunk back. Perrier bent down, straightened with the wolf's brush in his hand and faced Dan Shea.

"Well run, sir!" he praised. "Well run. The brush is yours, Mr Shea."

Dan took the brushy tail. He found that he was panting, that he felt as though he had undergone heavy exertion. "Thanks," he said.

Perrier's eyes were dancing. "I've been master and huntsman too," he announced. "Now I've found a man to ride with me. Mr Shea, I congratulate you."

Side by side, the dogs following, the two rode back across the hill. The horses were wet with sweat, but still Dan could feel the tremendous force, the steel springs that were beneath him. Neither man spoke until the camp was reached. Then, when they had dismounted and the silent Robert came to take the horses, Perrier faced his companion.

"I think I understand now," he said, his eyes sparkling.

"Understand what?" Dan asked.

"Why the dogs came to you last night. You're a gentleman, Mr Shea."

Dan made no answer, and Perrier shook his head. "But you must be better mounted," he continued. "That horse you have . . . he won't do, Mr Shea. He won't do at all!"

CHAPTER SIX:

RIDER AFOOT

Perrier stayed at Rancho Norte for three days. Dan did not again hunt with the Englishman although Perrier pressed him to go. There was too much work, too much business for Dan Shea to attend, and he could not spare the time. He acted as his own *caporal*, shifting his flocks from grazing to grazing, taking supplies to the camps of his herders, attending the work. At the end of the three days Perrier departed, Robert driving the wagon that was the Englishman's home, the spare horses following the wagon, the dogs behind the horses and Perrier, mounted on the big bay, bringing up the rear. Before he left Perrier promised to come back, and his blue eyes were warm as he made the promise. Puck and Mab, dignified as became their royal blood, accepted Dan's parting caress, and Mab touched his hand with her tongue.

When Perrier was gone Dan was singularly lonely. He had not been with the Englishman a great deal, and yet Perrier had afforded a certain companionship, just his presence making itself felt at Rancho Norte. But work pressed, and Dan Shea had no time for solitude as he plunged into his tasks.

In moving the sheep over the grass Dan covered all the range of Rancho Norte. To the north El Puerto del Sol was bounded by the little stream upon which the house was located. This creek, Rito Osos, bent away toward the northeast, its headwaters in the Alforjas. As summer came and the rains held off the stream died, becoming a series of potholes in the stream bed. So, too, as the spring drought grew, the other water died; the little springs along the Alforjas, the water holes in the range, one by one emptied and turned into dry beds of cracked mud.

There were cattle north of Rito Osos. Occasionally Dan Shea, moving his sheep, saw cows. Once or twice he saw riders in the distance, but neither cattle nor riders encroached upon the range south of the creek.

Wary of the season, and with the knowledge of Hilario and Martin O'Connor to aid him, Dan saved the grass along the creek. Always through late May and early June the country was dry. July brought rain in the hills and refreshed the streams and the grass, but July was not yet. So utilizing the southern portion of his range, Dan gradually brought his bands toward the north where Rito Osos would furnish water and the grass he had saved would give feed to tide over the dry period. By the end of May the lambs were docked and altered and the sheep were congregated along the creek. Don Martin O'Connor, visiting his *partidario* at Rancho Norte, had a report of range, of water and of the position of the flocks and was well pleased.

O'Connor did not stay the night. Dan's house, under construction by Hilario's cousin, was not yet ready for occupancy although the walls were going up in good fashion. O'Connor looked over the work but grinned and shook his head when Dan suggested that he stay.

"I'll not put you out of your bed," O'Connor said, "an' I'm too old to sleep on the ground with the sky for a blanket. I'll go home." Accordingly, he climbed into his buckboard and drove away, and Dan, watching him, remembered suddenly that he had not asked concerning Marillita. He comforted himself with the knowledge that Don Martin would have mentioned it had the girl been ill or absent and, when the *patrón* was out of sight, went back to work.

The day following O'Connor's departure Dan rode north along Rito Osos. Some eight miles from Rancho Norte he stopped his horse. Agapito Bargas, Hilario's youngest son, should have been holding a band of sheep at this spot, but neither sheep nor Agapito were in evidence. Instead there were cattle grazing on the good grass that Dan Shea had saved. Anger, hot and sudden, filled Dan, and he rode down upon the cattle.

Gathering them, he drove them back across Rito Osos, dry at this point, and when he had given the cows and calves a shove out upon the northern side of the creek went back and, riding to the highest point immediately available, searched the country with his eyes. Below him, perhaps a mile distant, he saw his sheep and, leaving his vantage point, Dan rode toward them.

Agapito and his dogs were with the flock. Agapito's camp with its hobbled burros was on a dry arroyo. Dan passed by the camp, noting its unfavorable position with a frown, and went on out to the sheep. Dismounting beside Agapito, he demanded sharply why the flock was not along Rito Osos.

Agapito gesticulated as he talked, and his voice was shrill as he answered Dan's question. Yesterday, Agapito said, three men, *tres hombres,* had ridden down upon him as he brought the sheep to water. They had cursed him and shown him guns. They had ordered him to leave the water and not spoil it with his stinking sheep. Agapito was frightened. He had moved his sheep back from Rito Osos. As Agapito's recital reached its climax Dan Shea's scowl deepened.

"Who were these men?" he demanded.

Agapito spread his hands wide. They had come from the north, he answered. *Vaqueros,* he thought.

"Move your band back to the creek," Dan ordered sternly. "I'll go and see these men."

Leaving Agapito uttering protests and warnings, Dan mounted and rode north.

He crossed the creek where he had found the cattle and, striking steadily northward, left the stream. The YH ran cattle north of the creek in a country that was new to Dan. He knew it only by hearsay and he had never met Jesse Louder who owned and operated the YH.

Traveling steadily, Dan crossed a wagon road. Surmising that the road would lead him to the YH headquarters, he turned east and followed it. Within two miles he saw smoke, and before another quarter mile was behind him he saw the buildings, the corrals and sheds of a cow outfit spread out in a draw. Dan rode down, stopped at the corral and demanded of the sleepy-eyed native who came shambling out of the barn the whereabouts of Señor Louder.

Louder, the native answered, was riding, but it was almost noon and he would be back at noon. Dan tied his horse to the corral fence and sat down, leaning against the barrier. He would, he said, wait for Louder.

Time dragged by and the sun was straight up at its zenith. Dan heard horses and voices and raised himself from beside the corral. A tall man, gaunt and with sweeping mustachios, accompanied by a shorter companion, was coming around the corner of the corral. The men stopped their horses and dismounted. Dan advanced toward them.

"Mr Louder?" he asked.

"I'm Louder," the tall man said. "What do you want?"

Dan surveyed the two men. The short rider with Louder was Buster, the drunken cowpuncher of Bendición. "I'm Shea," Dan said curtly. "I'm running sheep on the north end of El Puerto del Sol. Yesterday three of your men came down on one of my herders and kicked him off the creek. This morning I found a bunch of YH cows using my grass. I came over to see you about it."

Deliberately Louder leaned his length against the fence and looked at Dan through narrow slitted eyes. Both riders were armed. Indeed, in that country it was seldom that an unarmed man was found on the range. Booted, spurred, the two cowmen made a contrast to Dan Shea. They were, they knew—as every cowman knew—the aristocracy of the range. They believed in their superiority and were arrogant in it.

"You work for O'Connor," Louder announced flatly. "I'll have no truck with any man that works for him. You can pull out, Shea."

Anger began to lift in Dan Shea. He stared steadily at Louder. "I work for myself," he announced. "It's my grass that you've been usin', not O'Connor's or anybody else's. It wasn't O'Connor that came to talk to you, Louder. It was me."

Somehow that got home to the cowman. There was a small frosty twinkle in his eyes. "All right," Louder agreed, "it was you that come. What are you goin' to do about it, Shea?"

"I'm going to push your cattle back on your side," Dan answered sturdily, "and I won't stand for you trying to run a blazer on my herders."

"We're out of water." Louder vouchsafed condescending explanation. "Your sheep stink up the holes along the creek till the cattle won't use 'em."

Dan made a swift decision in his mind. He knew that Louder was right on that count; the cattle would not water where the sheep had drunk and muddied the water holes.

"My sheep are north of Rancho Norte," he said. "I'll keep them there. There's plenty of water in the creek south of the ranch. You use the south end and I'll use the north, and we won't come together."

It was a fair offer and both men knew it. But Dan Shea was a sheepman, and Louder handled cattle. Between the two stretched all the distance of the ages, the difference of the man who works on foot and the man who rides a horse. Jesse Louder would not condescend to treaty.

"I'll think about it," he drawled.

"I've thought about it," Dan Shea said. "It goes like I've said. And the grass south of the creek is mine. Keep your cattle on your side."

Buster, since his advent, had scowled steadily at Dan Shea. Now he put in his oar. "You're mighty uppity for a sheepherder," he snapped. "I ain't drunk today. Mebbe . . ."

"Shut up, Buster." Louder's voice was calm. He faced Dan, and again his eyes encompassed the man. "What would you do if I didn't keep my cows north of the creek?" he demanded levelly.

Dan grinned. He was hot inside, filled with anger and ready to fight, but good fighting man that he was, he recognized that the time for battle was not yet.

"If I made a threat you'd shove your cows over to see if I'd keep it." He answered Louder's question. "I don't know what I'd do, Mr Louder."

Louder's thin smile showed beneath his mustache. "Mebbe I'll just shove 'em across anyhow," he drawled. "You've made a big talk, Shea."

"I've made a fair proposition," Dan answered.

"Mebbe."

"I'll leave it with you." Dan turned toward his horse and, reaching up, untied the reins.

These men were enemies through tradition, but Jesse Louder had been brought up in the Southwestern school of unfailing courtesy. Friend or enemy, Louder would not turn a man away at meal-time.

"It's dinnertime, Shea," he said. "You'd better stay an' see what the cook's got."

"Thanks," Dan answered, "but I've got to get back."

Courtesy had been offered as was commanded. Too, it had been refused, as etiquette dictated. Louder said: "Suit yourself," without inflection, and Dan Shea, leading his horse away from the corral, mounted and, not looking back, rode south.

For the next two days Dan patrolled the creek, watching the grass on his side of the stream, keep-

ing his sheep east of the house as he had offered.
On the third day, riding out just after sunup, he
found a little bunch of cows, about fifty head, on
the south side of the creek, and they were not five
miles east of his headquarters. It was apparent then
to Dan Shea that Louder had not taken his offer;
that Louder, with the contempt of the cowman for
the sheepman, was infringing on Dan's grass.

Dan had made an offer to Louder and he had
also made some fighting talk. If he let this go he
was licked. It was up to Dan to back his talk or get
out. The latter idea did not enter his mind. Anger
seethed in him as he threw the fifty head of cows
together. Louder wanted the grass south of the
creek. All right. Dan would give him plenty of that
grass. Instead of pushing the cattle back across the
creek and turning them loose there, Dan fell in
behind them and drove southeast, toward the rug-
ged canyons of the Alforjas. There was grass in the
Alforjas, but there was no water at this season. Dan
planned to put the YH cows that had been thrown
on his grass some fifteen miles up in the Alforjas.
Then Louder could look for them if he wanted to.

Within fifteen minutes of his decision Dan had
the cows gathered and strung out and was pushing
right along behind them. South of Rito Osos the
country rolled away, a bench land, higher than the
stream and bisected by small canyons that cut down
through the bench to carry floodwater to the creek.
Dan Shea and the cattle entered one of these small
folds, Dan behind the cows. He was in the canyon
and the cattle were climbing the slope when, from
above and to the right, a rifle sounded. Dan's horse,
hit behind the shoulder, the bullet striking in
through the front jockey of the saddle, staggered

and went down, and Dan had barely time enough to throw himself clear before the horse struck the ground.

Momentarily Dan Shea was dazed by the fall. He lay where he had fallen, his head swimming. Then he pulled himself up, a movement that saved his life. There was a sharp spang of sound, and gravel leaped from where his body had rested, while a bullet ricocheted away, whining. On the hill to the right a puff of smoke went up and drifted away on the wind.

Dan Shea dropped and rolled to his horse. The horse had fallen on his left side, and the butt of Dan's Sharps was upthrust on the right side of the saddle. Lying flat against the dead horse, Dan reached for the Sharps and possessed himself of the rifle.

The Sharps was a .45–.110, a relic of the days when Dan Shea had hunted buffalo. It weighed some twelve pounds, and there was a peep sight on the tang of the action. Dan pushed the peep sight up, cocked the Sharps and, squirming around so that he could rest the barrel on the horse's flank, sent a five-hundred-grain slug up the hillside. Rock spurted up from the base of a yucca clump; the smoke drifted off, and Dan peered over his barricade.

The hillside was lifeless. Dan slid another shell into the greasy, smoking breech of the Sharps and waited.

He was not in a very good spot. Immobilized because of the death of his horse, down below his hidden attacker, he was open to assault from three directions. The man who had shot at him could shift north or south; he could even circle and get to the east. Any one of those movements would expose Dan and make his position untenable. All of these things Dan knew and could not alter. The cows had moved off up the canyon and were grazing unconcernedly on the slopes. The sun was getting higher and hotter, and all across the canyon quiet prevailed.

There was not much hope of rescue. Dan's *pastores* were with his herds and none were close. Had they been, he might have had some help for, save for Agapito, the men with the sheep were good sturdy citizens who would hold their own in almost any company. It looked like a tight spot to Dan Shea as he stared at the hillside above him.

Detecting small motion toward his right, Dan pulled the gun around. He wanted a target. Give him a glimpse of a man through his sights and he would be satisfied. The motion proved to be caused by a small bird that flitted out of a yucca and flew away, and Dan grunted. Distinctly it was his move and, equally distinctly, a move might be disastrous. There was not too much patience in Dan Shea. This was not his kind of fight. He preferred action. Cautiously he gathered himself. He would bob up and drop down. Up on the hill the man might have unsteady nerves. A hasty shot would at least locate Dan's assailant. That the same hasty shot might put a period to the fight did not enter Dan Shea's mind. He came up like a jack-in-the-box, appearing momentarily above the body of the horse and then, equally swift, dropped into concealment again.

The ruse worked. On the hill the dry gulcher

pulled his trigger. Dan did not hear the solid thump of lead into his horse's belly. He drowned that sound with the roar of the Sharps. From above two small rocks, just at the top of the ridge, smoke drifted away and Dan Shea sent the slugs from the Sharps searching about the stones. He fired three times and paused, not sure of the effects of his shooting, waiting and listening, trying to detect his results, if any.

Again silence hung over the draw, the dead horse, the man and the cattle. Dan, with the Sharps ready, searched the ridge with his eyes. Then there was a scurrying movement, and the Sharps kicked back sharply against his shoulder.

The crash of the rifle rang in Dan's ears as he reloaded. He squirmed for better position, saw a mounted man atop the hill, leveled the Sharps again and, miraculously, stayed his finger on the trigger. The mounted man was coming along the ridge at a run, arm thrust out as he leaned forward on his horse. The rider was shooting at something in front of him. Dan stood up.

On top of the ridge the rider disappeared. Two reports, the first one loud, the second fainter, drifted back to Dan. With the rifle dangling in his hand Shea started up the ridge.

He was on top, surveying the country to the west, when he saw a horseman coming toward him. The rider came deliberately, as though in no hurry. Dan sat down to wait. Either this approaching rider was the man who had driven off Dan's attacker or he might possibly be the dry gulcher himself. In either event Dan was prepared. Sitting there on the ridge top, he waited.

The rider came on, his horse climbing. When he

was close enough Dan identified the man. Jesse Louder was coming toward him. Louder's horse was sweating, and Louder himself showed some excitement. He stopped beside Dan, dismounted and stood looking down. "You hurt?" Louder asked.

"No," Dan answered. "My horse is dead."

"He was up here in the rocks," Louder announced. "I heard the shootin' an' I came across the creek to see what it was. I saw him an' I saw his horse. He heard me comin', I guess. Anyhow, he lit a shuck for his horse an' pulled out. I couldn't catch him." There was regret in the cowman's voice.

Deliberately Dan lowered the hammer of the Sharps, rested it across his knees and reached into the pocket of his vest for tobacco and papers. "I thought it might be some of you folks," he drawled, looking searchingly at Louder. "I found a bunch of your cattle on my grass and I was moving them."

Louder advanced a step and looked down the slope of the ridge. Dan's dead horse lay in the bottom of the draw. The cattle grazed along the slopes. Anger glinted in Louder's eyes.

"Where did you figure to take them cows?" he demanded.

"Back into the hills," Dan answered calmly. "I'd made you a fair proposition, Louder. It looked to me like you'd called my hand."

Louder frowned. "Come on," he ordered abruptly. "I want to look at this."

Dan got up. Louder mounted. With the cowman riding and Dan walking beside him, they went back down the hill.

Louder did not bother with the cattle. He turned toward Rito Osos. Dan said nothing but walked along beside the horse. When they reached the creek Dan stopped. Louder rode over to the stream, worked along the bank, east and west, stopped, apparently to examine something, and then came slowly back to the man on foot.

"They were shoved across," Louder said slowly. "I found horse tracks."

Dan nodded, watching Louder's angry eyes.

"I gave orders," Louder said, staring at Dan, "for the stuff up here to be drifted west. I'd decided to take your proposition, Shea."

Still Dan waited, making no comment. Louder was frowning. He shifted his eyes from Dan's.

"I'll push those cattle back," he announced suddenly. "You want me to side you back home? Do you want to take your saddle in?"

"No," Dan replied and then, warmth in his voice: "I'm obliged to you, Louder. That fellow had me treed."

Jesse Louder grinned. The smile drove all the coldness from his face and warmed it. "I expect I'd of done the same thing you did," he said. "It would have been tough for me to find them cows back in the hills though."

"I wanted to make it tough." Dan answered Louder's smile with one of his own. "I thought you'd decided to run a blazer on me. I was going to take you up on it."

"I don't think," Louder said, "that you'll find any more YH cows on your grass, Shea. If you do they'll be strays, an' I'll be obliged if you'll just push 'em back."

"Why sure," Dan agreed. "If they're west of the house it won't make any difference anyhow. I'm not going to use that grass there till later. After it rains."

For a moment neither man spoke, then Louder shifted his weight in his saddle and his horse moved. "If you don't want me to take your saddle in I'll pick up the cows an' go on," he drawled. "I've got a little business to tend to back at the ranch."

"I'll send out for the saddle," Dan replied. "I'm much obliged to you, Louder."

"That's all right," Louder answered. The horse turned. Louder rode up the draw toward the grazing cattle. Dan Shea watched him for a moment and then, lifting the heavy Sharps until it rested across his arm, started down the creek toward Rancho Norte.

In the next three days Dan Shea, riding his retrieved saddle on a fresh horse, saw movement across the creek. At the end of the three days when he rode east from Rancho Norte and looked to the north he saw no cattle. The country east of Rancho Norte and north of the creek had been cleaned of cows. West of the ranch, however, there were plenty of cattle. Dan grinned as he came home.

On the fourth day following the trouble Dan, coming in from his herds, found that he had a visitor at the ranch. Fitzpatrick, tall and sandy and smiling, met Dan as he dismounted.

When the men had shaken hands Fitzpatrick drawled: "I thought I'd come out an' see how you were makin' it."

"I'm mighty glad you came," Dan replied. "Come on. We'll clean up and see what Domisinda's got to eat."

After supper, sitting in front of Dan Shea's new rock house, Fitzpatrick talked. His cigar smoldering, peacefully stretched out with his shoulders against the new rock wall, he came to the purpose of his visit.

"There's quite some talk in town," Fitzpatrick said. "Seems like you had some trouble out here."

"How did you hear about it?" Dan asked.

A smile lined Fitzpatrick's face. "Buster Flint is in town," he drawled. "He's been drinkin' quite a little. Seems like Buster is pretty sore about Louder firing him because of a sheepman."

"So?" Dan said. So it had been Buster that pushed the YH cattle across the creek! And Louder had fired Buster because of the incident.

"Buster's cussin' Jesse Louder," Fitzpatrick continued. "He's pretty sore. He says it's too bad you wasn't killed instead of your horse."

"You heard about that too?"

"Buster's got quite a tale. Mebbe it ain't all so. What happened, Dan?"

Dan puffed the cigar that Fitzpatrick had given him. "I'll tell you what happened," he agreed.

When he had completed his story there was a pause; then into the quiet Fitzpatrick dropped soft words.

"It might be that was some my fault," he said. "You see, I told Youtsey about you seein' one of them fello's that killed Maples there in town."

"Yes?" Dan prompted.

"Yeah. I told him about that an' about how the fello' was talkin' to George Delaney. It might just be, Dan . . ."

"It might be what?"

"It might be that Youtsey asked Delaney about who he'd been talkin' to. An' it might be that Delaney saw the same man again. An' then, you bein' able to recognize him an' all, it might be that that fello' thought you were a little dangerous. I'm kind of watchin' out for things myself. I keep my eyes open. It would pay you to do the same thing, I think."

There was a long silence. Then: "It's an idea, anyhow," Dan Shea said.

Fitzpatrick, having delivered his message and warning, turned to other subjects. "Youtsey," he commented, drawing smoke from his cigar, "has been doin' himself some good. He found out who that fello' was that was killed at San Felice."

"So?"

"Uh-huh. We knew his name was Maples, but Youtsey's been writin' to the capital. Maples run a little abstract office up there. Kind of a jackleg. Made abstracts, sold some real estate, done a lot of things."

"And so?" Dan prompted.

"An' so Youtsey's got his mystery solved. He knows just who was murdered."

"But not who did the murdering."

"No." Fitzpatrick contemplated his cigar again. "He ain't got that far with it yet. Youtsey is easy satisfied."

Dan Shea grunted. "We gave him descriptions of the men who did the killing," he commented. "It looks like he might have gone along with that end first."

"Them men are alive," Fitzpatrick said succinctly. "They might still do some shootin'. Now Maples is dead an' buried. He's *safe* to investigate."

Again Dan grunted and Fitzpatrick puffed on his cigar. Their unspoken opinion of the sheriff of Seco County hung heavy between them. It was not a good opinion.

CHAPTER SEVEN:
THERE GOLD IS FOUND

In the first week of June the shearers came to Rancho Norte. They camped along the creek, and there their cooking fire was built. Daily Dan's herders brought in sheep, and daily, in the long shed set in the center of the corrals, the shearers worked. They were men apart from all others, skilled workmen, under the orders of a *capitán* with whom Dan had made his bargain. The shearers, the *llaneros* who packed the wool into sacks, even the *colero*—the boy who carried the bucket of thin tar to daub on wounds made by slipping shears—did not consort with the men of El Puerto del Sol. They formed a clan of their own. But even clansmen fight among themselves, and on the third day of shearing at Rancho Norte there was trouble in the shearers' camp.

Dan Shea had moved into his new rock house. It was not entirely finished but was better than the tent. Lounging in a rawhide-bottomed homemade chair, resting from the day's work, he heard the trouble start. Angry voices came through the dusk. For a moment Dan listened, and then as one voice changed from harsh anger to shrill terror he sprang up and ran in the direction of the sound.

When he reached the camp he found the shearers crowded around the fire. Fire and twilight made them bulk black, and Dan, thrusting through the men, entered a cleared space. On one side of the clearing the boy—the *colero*—was crouched, frightened, evidently, but in his fright ready to fight. Across from him was a shearer, a pock-marked, burly man whom Dan had noted as the most careless and the slowest of the shearers. The pock-marked man was scowling. He did not note Dan's arrival but, cautious as some stalking cat, advanced on the boy, a knife in his upthrust hand and maledictions coming in a muttered stream from between his snarling lips.

Dan Shea did not hesitate. He did not know the right or wrong of the situation but he did know that the boy was small and the man burly. "¡Párelo, hombre!" Dan snapped.

The pock-marked man threw a glance over his shoulder, snarled a curse and took another step toward the boy. Dan Shea, nothing loath, closed in. He struck twice, sure and certain, dodging the knife before he struck the second blow. The knife, released, flew high and glittered in the firelight as it fell, and Dan Shea, body a straight line from heel to right fist, placed his third blow on the pock-marked jaw, just on angle. Lightning could have been no more thorough. The pock-marked man went down. The boy scurried out, dropping on hands and knees to scuttle between the legs of the men. Dan Shea stood, feet widespread, and addressed the shearing crew. When he finished the pock-marked man was sitting up, and there was no doubt in the mind of any of his hearers that Señor Dan Shea would not stand for foolishness on Rancho Norte.

In the morning the pock-marked man was gone from the shearing shed. The men worked with more vigor when Dan Shea appeared, and Vicente Lebya, the *colero*, followed him around during all his visit, frank and almost embarrassing adoration in his eyes.

Stopping briefly beside the *capitán*, Dan spoke concerning the absence of the pock-marked man. The *capitán* shrugged his shoulders eloquently. "Hee's gone," the *capitán* said, and then, eying Dan narrowly: "He is a bad man, señor. Arturo de la Luz. He hass killed a man. You better be careful."

Dan grinned and nodded. "I'll watch out," he said, and then: "This bunch is shearing a little lighter than those we had yesterday."

The shearers stayed a week at Rancho Norte. At the end of that time all of Dan Shea's sheep were sheared, and some of the wool had been hauled away in the creaking wagons that Don Martin had sent from El Puerto del Sol. Don Martin had bought wool from Dan in addition to taking his own part of the shear. With the money the *patrón* paid him, Dan had paid his shearers. Some small amount yet remained, as well as the greater part of his wool. For the first time since his arrival at Bendición Dan began to feel like a capitalist.

One of the shearing crew did not leave the *rancho*. Vincent Lebya, the *colero*, stayed on, nor could Dan Shea's amused assurance that there was no work, or the positive hostility of Hilario and his family, drive the boy away. Perforce Dan fed him, and Vicente, finding a place to sleep in one of the sheds, bared the knife he had retrieved on the night of the fight and drove Hilario away when Hilario came to remonstrate.

There was something odd about the boy, something that was not true to the native type as Dan had come to know it, and when Hilario, wrathful and breathing threats and desires of vengeance, came to Dan demanding that Vicente be ordered to leave Dan did not accede. Instead he went to the shed, called Vicente and brought the boy out into the light.

Under questioning Vicente gave reluctant information. He had no family. He was an orphan. He had no home. He had no relatives. Hilario, standing by, grunted scornfully and spoke his mind: "¡Es indio!"

The boy's black eyes flashed vengefully at the speaker, and Dan knew that Hilario had been right. Vicente was an Indian.

"Apache?" Dan demanded sharply.

Vicente did not answer for a moment, and then reluctantly he nodded. Dan turned to Hilario. "Let him stay," he directed. "And feed him."

Light filled Vicente's eyes, and Hilario, muttering to himself, stamped away. From that time on about Rancho Norte Dan Shea had a second shadow, a boy who moved wraithlike at his heels, watching him with black, adoring eyes.

Following the shearing there was a respite in the work at Rancho Norte. There came a change in the weather too. Clouds gathered about the tops of the Alforjas, bunched and grew black. Rain fell, making of Rito Osos a torrent, filling the water holes, giving new life to the burned grass. Rain brings relief to the range country, rejuvenates it and lifts the hearts of men. There was a week of rain, and at the end of the week Dan Shea stood and watched lambs playing, and he laughed aloud with no one to hear him. It was good to be alive, good to be relieved of restraint, good to be young and strong and working, building for a future.

All across the range country, all through the pastures of the YH, through El Puerto del Sol, that feeling spread so that when Dan, on impulse, saddled a horse and rode south to visit Don Martin he found the spirit of fiesta imbuing the little settlement below the hacienda.

At the house itself Don Martin greeted him jovially and Marillita came smiling to bid him welcome. There was a feast that night: young mutton, vegetables from the gardens, fine bread and *biscochos* and wine, and when the meal was done Don Martin sat awhile with the two young people and then, pleading his need for rest, betook himself to his room, leaving Dan and Marillita alone in the patio.

They sat upon the bench while the moon came up to look down into the patio and while the mocking-bird that had built a nest in the cottonwood sang in the moonlight. Marillita did not whistle to the bird, and Dan sat silent, listening to the song, and presently he felt the soft fingers of the girl's hand slipped into his own hard palm.

The following morning Dan Shea went out with Martin O'Connor, returning again at night. Two days he stayed at El Puerto del Sol, returning to Rancho Norte on the third day. When he was gone Marillita moped about the house, her spirits fallen, and Don Martin O'Connor, smiling slyly, spoke at length concerning his *partidario* on Rancho Norte, doubting Dan's ability to be successful in the partnership and hurrying away so that he might laugh when Marillita rose hotly to Dan's defense.

Who knows the way of a man with a woman? Who can fathom the season when life, refreshed by rain, stirs all across the range country and a man's blood runs hot? Dan Shea, at Rancho Norte, was preoccupied and dissatisfied. Marillita, at El Puerto del Sol, was given to long silences wherein she did not hear her father's words.

There was a distance between Rancho Norte and El Puerto del Sol, a weary travel. To Dan Shea the distance south grew great and the journey north a plague. At first it was once a week that he made the trip, dropping down from Rancho Norte to spend the Sunday with Martin O'Connor. Then the visits grew more frequent and the intervals between them less until all El Puerto del Sol grinned and, with affection, spoke of Danielito and his courtship.

So July came to an end.

In August, with the heat oppressive during the day, with the rains breaking the heat, with the grass growing green all across the range land, Dan Shea stood at the house of El Puerto del Sol and watched a band of sheep coming into the corrals below the house. Martin O'Connor, coming up from the pens, stood beside Dan and also watched the sheep. O'Connor was dusty, and streaks of sweat beaded his forehead when he pushed back his hat.

"We're goin' to separate 'em," he said. "I want the wethers out of there."

Dan nodded absently. "Where's Marillita?" he asked.

"Look at the sheep a minute," O'Connor commanded.

Dan looked at the sheep. O'Connor placed his

hand on Dan's shoulder. "That's what makes El Puerto del Sol," he said. "Sheep."

He was silent a moment and then spoke again. "My wife's people have a saying: *'El pie de la oveja siempre deja oro.'* I guess it's true."

"Wherever the sheep sets his hoof, there gold is found," Dan interpreted automatically.

"El Puerto has always been sheep." O'Connor's hand remained on Dan's shoulder. "Come on in and sit down, Dan."

Dan followed O'Connor into the patio. There on a bench beside Don Martin's bulk he seated himself. O'Connor relaxed, leaning back.

"Dan," he said abruptly, "there's a cure for what ails you."

"Nothing ails me!" Dan refuted. "I . . ." He stopped, sensing rather than seeing the laughter that was in Martin O'Connor's eyes. There was a thing that ailed Dan Shea, a thing that tormented him. Dan knew it.

O'Connor teetered his bulk on the bench. "There's two parts to a man's business," he said abruptly. "First there's his livin'. He's got to work at that because a man without work is a husk of a man. There's no meat to the kernel of him. An' then there's the rest of a man." O'Connor's voice grew soft. "He can build himself a place an' have his work an' all of that an' still not be a whole man because he lacks somethin'. You lack somethin', Dan Shea!"

O'Connor paused. When he spoke again his voice was softer still. "When I was young I lacked somethin' too. I found it an' then I lost it: Marillita's mother. She was what I lacked an' what I lost. But I'd had her, Dan. She'd been mine. Do you know what I mean?"

There was a long silence in the patio. Dan Shea did not answer. Martin O'Connor hoisted himself from the bench. "Well," he said prosaically, "I've got to separate them sheep." He strode away, leaving Dan alone.

Overhead the sun was bright, and the patio was quiet in the heat. There was a movement that Dan did not detect, and then the bench where Martin O'Connor had sat was occupied again. Dan, reaching out his hand, found another hand placed within it. For a time longer he sat there, not turning, simply holding that other hand in his own, and then he spoke, his voice hoarse with the thing that was in his mind.

"Marillita?"

"Yes, Dan?"

Again a moment's silence. Then: "I love you, Marillita," Dan Shea said. "I'm half a man. Will you make me a whole one?"

The hand that Dan Shea held turned slowly until the palm was uppermost. Marillita did not speak. The small hand closed and Dan Shea turned. The girl was looking at him, her eyes brave and direct, and in them was his answer. Dan freed his hand and reached out his arms, and as she moved toward him the sunlight, bright and glinting, caught in her hair and turned it all to gold. And then that golden head was against Dan's chest and Marillita's face was hidden from his eyes and his arms were tight about her. Dan Shea had found his gold.

They were still on the bench when Martin O'Connor came back from the pens. The big man paused in the patio gate and surveyed the scene, the little plot of grass, the shade of the cottonwood, the flowers that bloomed along the wall, the two on the bench, man and woman, self-conscious as children before his gaze. Big and formidable, his legs widespread, his blue eyes questioning, Don Martin stood there.

Then Marillita left the bench and, running to her father, threw her arms about his neck and kissed him, and Dan Shea, rising awkwardly, approached the two.

"I . . ." he began. "Don Martin, I . . ."

Martin O'Connor freed one hand from his daughter's shoulders and reached it out to Dan Shea.

"I'll trust her to you, Dan," Don Martin said. "She's the best I have, but I'll trust her to you."

And now a busy time came to El Puerto del Sol. At Rancho Norte the carpenters and masons put the final touches to Dan Shea's new rock house, building another room and completing those already built. At the hacienda of El Puerto del Sol the women began their bustling. Dan Shea, Marillita and Martin O'Connor, consulting together, had set the wedding date for fall. When the sheep had gone to market and when the work was through, there at the harvesttime was the time for weddings, Don Martin said, and Dan, impatient, perforce agreed. All across the grant, from the great house and the little settlement, on to the camps of the *pastores*, to the small houses of the *partidarios*, the word spread and El Puerto del Sol blossomed and made plans and groomed itself.

Dan Shea moved in a daze. He went about his work at Rancho Norte with but half his mind attending to his tasks. Marillita, beautiful, gained more beauty with her love. Martin O'Connor was expansive and happy. The month of August waned.

Then in early September, riding toward El Puerto's hacienda, impatient with his horse's slowness, Dan Shea saw a rider coming toward him. The rider came on apace through the heat of the afternoon and, drawing close, Dan recognized Youtsey, the sheriff from Bendición. He drew rein as Youtsey came up, and the officer likewise halted. The greetings they exchanged were courteous and brief. Youtsey asked Dan Shea if he had seen Louder of the YH, and when Dan answered that he had not Youtsey spoke his good-by and rode on. Curiosity piquing him, Dan, too, resumed his journey.

Marillita met him at the door when Dan dismounted. Her face showed anxiety, and her kiss was brief. Dan held the girl at arm's length.

"What's the matter, dearest?" he asked.

Marillita shook her head. "Father's in his room, Dan," she answered. "Something's happened. You'd better go to him."

Leaving the girl, Dan sought O'Connor. The big man was in the room where the business of El Puerto del Sol was transacted. His eyes were angry and his cheeks were flushed. For the first time Dan Shea saw the hard, ruthless man who in all the Bendición country had no friends. O'Connor rose as Dan came in, papers grasped in his great fist.

"Youtsey was here," O'Connor rumbled. "I'd have sent for you if I hadn't known you were comin'."

"I passed Youtsey going north," Dan said calmly. "What's wrong, Don Martin?"

Fist and papers came down with a thump upon the table top. "You're with me in this, Dan!" O'Connor growled. "They're at it again. By God, this time I'll go through with it. I'll kill the dirty devils. Tryin' to take El Puerto! They can't do it. They can't have any part of it. I tell you . . ."

Dan Shea broke into the tirade, his calm voice cutting into O'Connor's anger like a knife.

"Sit down, Don Martin," he commanded.

O'Connor's voice checked, and he stared at Dan Shea in bewilderment.

Dan held out his hand. "Before I get into a fight," he said easily, "I want to know who I'm fighting an' why. Sit down an' tell me about it. Let's see what you've got there."

Like a child stopped in the midst of a tantrum, Martin O'Connor sat down and, reaching out, laid the crumpled papers in Dan's outstretched hand.

CHAPTER EIGHT:

DISPUTED TITLE

The papers that Dan Shea received from O'Connor
were a complaint and a summons. Ramon de la
Luz, in company with others of his clan, was seeking satisfaction from Martin O'Connor and Jesse
Louder, so the complaint read. The complaint
stated that O'Connor had sold a portion of the
grant to Louder; that he had no right to make that
sale for he held no title to the land; that the title
was vested in a grant given to one Selberio de la
Luz by Francisco Cuervo, governor general of New
Mexico, in the days when all of Mexico belonged to
Spain. Ramon de la Luz and all other of Selberio's
heirs prayed redress from Martin O'Connor and
were suing for that redress.

Having finished reading, Dan looked up at Martin O'Connor. "Suppose," he drawled, "that you tell
me about it, Don Martin."

O'Connor, his anger ebbing before a sympathetic
listener, rasped out words. The tale was complex
enough, but simple in the telling. El Puerto del Sol
had been given to an early Alarid by Philip of Spain
himself. The Alarids had held it. Then later, at the
end of the Spanish occupancy, Cuervo, as governor
general, had given land to Selberio de la Luz. Some

of that land had lain across the grant of El Puerto del Sol. The Alarids and the De la Luzes had gone to court. The viceroy had appointed a judge, and when the trial was done El Puerto del Sol belonged to the Alarids and the De la Luz grant had been changed to land along the river.

Dan listened gravely to Don Martin's tale. There were many angry interruptions, many wrathful interjections. Through these Dan followed the thread of the story. When it was done Dan sat, thoughtful, while Martin O'Connor watched him.

This was his battle, just as it was Don Martin's. Now Dan could feel the grip of El Puerto del Sol; now he could feel its hold upon him. He was tied, bound to the grant. Nothing that affected El Puerto but that affected him also. Chains held him to the place. His love for Marillita, his affection for Martin O'Connor, his stake at Rancho Norte: all these were the chains. But more than these, stronger and greater than any or all of them, was El Puerto del Sol itself. Dan Shea looked up and met Don Martin's eyes.

"There's been a settlement," he said. "We've no cause for worry. What we need is a lawyer, a good sharp man that can find the records and settle this. We'll get one, Don Martin."

"But the nerve of them La Luzes!" Don Martin snapped. "The very nerve of them. There's always been a fight between the La Luzes an' the Alarids. I've had some trouble in my time with them. An' now they bring this up, just when you an' Marillita are gettin' married an' all. By God, I could kill the man that . . ."

Dan laughed. "You'll have to go to Albuquerque to get your lawyer," he said. "Marillita told me the last time I was here that she wanted to go to the pueblo to buy some things. We'll mix business with pleasure, Don Martin, an' take the trip together."

Martin O'Connor could not restrain a laugh with Dan. Good humor—ever close to the surface in the big man, just as anger was ever close—rose up to drown the anger. "Why," said Martin O'Connor, "we can make a party of it, Dan. That's what we'll do. Let's get the girl in now an' make our plans."

Dan called Marillita into the room. The girl came hesitantly. When she saw Don Martin's face her own brightened and her trepidation vanished. O'Connor drew his daughter down upon his knee and gently pinched her firm chin with a big forefinger and thumb.

"We're goin' to Albuquerque, Dan an' me," he boomed. "Do you think now that you could look after things whilst we're gone?"

Anger glinted in Marillita's eyes. "Look after things?" she snapped. "If you and Dan go to Albuquerque and leave me here you needn't look for me when you come back. I'll . . . I'll . . ."

O'Connor's laughter boomed. "In that case mebbe we'd best take you along," he said when the laughter was finished. "Mebbe it would be safer."

"You're trying to tease me," Marillita accused. "Father, I never thought it of you. You don't love me, either one of you."

It was the girl's turn to tease, and she made the most of it, hiding her face in her hands and weeping realistically. Dan sprang up and O'Connor, alarmed, sought to placate his daughter. It was not until he saw the corners of her lips and noted that they were upturned that Dan realized Marillita was retaliating. Then the farce was over and, laughing, the three sat down and planned the journey.

Nothing was said to Marillita as to the cause of O'Connor's trip. She hinted concerning the sudden decision, but her father gave no answer. It was not until later, when they were alone, that Dan told the girl the reason. Marillita was grave.

"I was afraid that there was trouble, Dan," she said. "You'll stay with Father, won't you? You won't let him do anything that he shouldn't?"

"Of course I'll stay with him," Dan assured. "It's just a legal matter. There's nothing to worry about, sweet."

Marillita laid her hand in Dan's. "All my life," she said, "I've seen trouble, Dan. It's only been these last few years that we've been free of it. Dan . . . when we're married there won't be any more trouble, will there?"

"None," Dan assured.

It seemed as though the girl did not hear that assurance. Her voice was musing. "Before I was born," she said, "when Father and Mother were first married, there was trouble at El Puerto del Sol. My grandfather had mortgaged the place. There were a lot of Alarids, Dan, and they all lived on the grant. All the cousins and second cousins and aunts and uncles and people that weren't relatives at all. And none of them were willing to help. They lived off the grant. Can you understand that, Dan?"

Dan nodded. He had seen just that thing happen, seen parasites prey upon a place until only a husk remained.

Marillita went on. "Dad married my mother and began to get things into his own hands. He sold some land and paid part of what was owed. He bought the interests of others. Some of them he sent away. Grandfather died, and my mother was the direct heir. And then I was born and my mother died. Father wanted to save the place for me. He fought for it, Dan."

Dan Shea listened in silence. He could see now why Martin O'Connor had the reputation of being a hard man, a ruthless man. It was necessary that he be hard and ruthless; essential that he put aside humanity in order to hold together the great domain that was El Puerto del Sol.

"Sometimes," Marillita said thoughtfully, "I don't think he did it for me or that he did it for my mother. I think he did it for El Puerto del Sol. It's kind of a religion with him, Dan. Ever since I was a little girl I can remember his talking to me, always talking about El Puerto del Sol and what it meant to him and what it must mean to me. He isn't like himself when somebody does something to El Puerto. He's like . . ." The girl paused, then: "He's like one of those ogres that I used to read about in fairy stories. He's . . . he's terrible, Dan."

The small hand that rested in Dan Shea's closed convulsively. "And he's old, Dan," the girl said. "I didn't know how old he was. He works terribly hard. And someday . . ."

"Marillita," Dan said earnestly, "you mustn't fret. You've got me now, and it's my business to keep trouble from you. I'll tend to it."

Marillita lifted her hand from Dan's, and her arms went about his neck. Her head against his chest, she murmured softly, "I feel so safe with you. Is it because I love you, Dan? Is it because . . . ?"

"It's because you *are* safe with me," Dan Shea

said. "Nothing will touch you, sweet. Nothing that I can prevent."

"What are you two talkin' about?" Martin O'Connor boomed from a doorway. "Plottin' against the old man, are you? I'll not have it. Not with me around. You'll have to take me into the plot."

Marillita lifted her head. "We were just thinking how long it is until October, Father," she answered. "And wishing that the days were shorter."

Later that day when O'Connor and Dan Shea sat talking together Jesse Louder came to El Puerto del Sol. He rode up on a sweating horse, stopping just at the great wooden gates that were opened into the patio, and with him were two hard-faced, lanky men who sat their horses and stared into the peace of the shaded enclosure.

Louder dismounted stiffly and came stalking forward, scowling. Behind him his two men also dismounted and, letting their horses stand, moved so that they were at either side of the patio gate, lounging beside the gateposts.

Martin O'Connor and Dan, rising, waited for Louder to approach. "Good day to you, Mr Louder," Don Martin greeted.

Louder did not respond to the salutation but plunged immediately into his errand. "Youtsey come to my place today," he announced. "Served these papers on me. I come to you about 'em, O'Connor."

"He was here too," O'Connor answered. "I've had a summons."

Louder spread out the complaint and summons, pulling them from his pocket. "I bought that country from you in good faith," he said belligerently.

"From what I read here you didn't have no right to sell it. I'm goin' to hold you responsible, O'Connor, an' if you've rooked me I'll . . ."

"What'll you do?" Don Martin snapped. "See here, Louder . . ." O'Connor's anger was rising and his voice was hostile. It was just as though two strange dogs had met and, snarling in preliminary, were ready to throw themselves at each other's throats.

"I'll . . ." Louder began, interrupting Don Martin.

"We've been talking about this, Mr Louder," Dan interposed quietly. "I'm glad that you've come over. Don Martin and I are going to Albuquerque to hire a lawyer to look into this for us."

Louder turned his angry eyes on Dan. "So you're in it too!" he snapped. "You told me that you didn't work for O'Connor."

"I don't," Dan answered levelly, keeping his temper in check. "But I'm interested. I've got sheep on shares with him, and my range comes under this suit."

"Why did they serve me?" Louder demanded, turning back to Don Martin. "I don't savvy. You sold me the land. It's up to you to make the title good."

"You'll not tell me what it's up to me to do!" O'Connor was red with his anger. "I know what I've got to do an' what I haven't. I . . ."

"Now wait!" Dan's calm voice cut into the tirade. "I'll tell you why you were served, Mr Louder. You're occupying part of the land that is included in the suit. That's why you were named and that's the only reason."

"I . . ." Louder began angrily.

"I'm not through," Dan interrupted. "Naturally

Mr O'Connor is going to defend himself. I told you that he was going to Albuquerque to hire a lawyer."

"I'll not put out a damned cent for this," Louder announced. "An' I tell you it won't be a lawsuit with me, O'Connor. You're responsible for the whole thing, and if there's trouble about it I'll . . ."

"You'll do what?" Martin O'Connor, thrusting his bulk ahead, shoved his face forward until it almost touched Louder's. "What'll you do?"

"I'll . . ."

"In a minute," Dan interposed coolly, "you'll both say something that you'll regret later. If you'll quit trying to fight each other and cool down a little you'll find out that you both want the same things. You're acting like a couple of fool kids."

Don Martin retreated a step and glared at Dan Shea. "A kid, am I?" he boomed. "I'll have you know . . ."

Dan's quiet eyes met those of the angry man, and O'Connor lapsed into silence. Dan turned and looked at Jesse Louder.

"You want title to your land," he said calmly. "That's all you want, isn't it, Mr Louder?"

"That's what I want," Louder rasped.

"And you want him to have it, Don Martin. You want to do the fair thing. Isn't that so?"

"I've never cheated a man in my life," Martin O'Connor rasped. "I sold the land in good faith. I'll make the title good."

"Then what are you fighting about?" Dan asked calmly. "You both want the same thing. Why fight? Why not help each other?"

As though the idea were totally new and strange to both of them Martin O'Connor and Jesse Louder stared at Dan Shea.

"We're going to Albuquerque," Dan continued. "We're going to hire a lawyer and clear this up. Don Martin's told me about the whole thing. There's nothing to worry about. This title has already been adjudicated. Don Martin had a right to sell it. This suit is just someone trying to stir up trouble. I tell you, Mr Louder, your title is good."

"You give me your word for that, Shea?" Louder demanded.

"I'll give you my word," Dan answered.

Louder pondered a moment. Then, lifting his eyes, he looked at Dan. "I'll take your word," he said bluntly. "I . . . I reckon I come over here half cocked, O'Connor. I was pretty well riled up." The apology was awkward. Don Martin, after a moment's pause, accepted the apology as awkwardly as it had been tendered.

"You an' me have had some trouble before," he said. "I don't know. Guess I'd of been riled too."

"Let's sit down and talk this out," Dan suggested.

Louder paused and then, looking toward his men at the gate, nodded to them. One man squatted beside the gate and the other collected the bridle reins of all three horses and led them out of the opening. Dan Shea, preceding O'Connor and Louder to a bench, sat down. When on either side of him the two men had placed themselves he spoke.

"Suppose you tell Mr Louder what you told me about this, Don Martin," he suggested.

O'Connor cleared his throat. "Well . . ." he began.

When Martin O'Connor's tale was done Louder nodded. "I see," he said. "An' now you're goin' to get a lawyer an' clear this up, is that it?"

"That's it," O'Connor rumbled.

Louder turned to Dan Shea. "All right," he said

grudgingly. "I guess you had the right of it. But I'll tell you both this: I'm not payin' a cent for the lawyer or for the courts."

"Nobody asked you to," O'Connor growled.

Louder stood up. Still looking at Dan, he spoke further. "You'll keep me posted?"

"I'll keep you posted," Dan assured. "It's about suppertime. You . . ."

"I'll go back to the ranch," Louder interrupted. "I mind one time I asked you to eat with me." He grinned suddenly.

Dan returned the smile. "You'd be welcome," he announced.

Louder stood up. "Maybe I would," he replied. "I'd better go home. Shea, you keep me posted, will you?"

"I'll keep you posted," Dan promised again.

Louder poised a moment, seemed about to say something more and then, forgoing the words, walked toward the gate. There his riders stood up and joined the cowman, and side by side they walked out of the gate and out of sight.

When the cowmen were gone there was quiet in the patio. Then Martin O'Connor said: "Danny, in another minute I'd of hit him. He come blusterin' an' blowin' in here an' . . ."

"It wouldn't have done any good, Don Martin," Dan Shea interrupted. "What would you have done if you'd been in his place?"

Martin O'Connor thought that over for some time. There was a sheepish expression on his face when he answered. "The same thing, I guess."

Preparations for the trip to Albuquerque filled the next few days. It was necessary before Martin

O'Connor and Dan Shea left El Puerto del Sol that everything be put in shape, that orders be given and that equipment be made ready. Don Martin would not go by stage. He had a canvas-covered, four-wheeled rig in which he purposed to make the trip. Marillita must have an ama; food and clothing must be made ready; there were many things to do. It was three days following Louder's visit to El Puerto del Sol before all was in readiness. On the morning of the fourth day, with Don Martin at the reins, with Marillita beside him and with a plump native woman on the back seat, the wagon rolled away from the hacienda. Dan Shea rode beside it.

Just after noon on the first day of the journey the spring wagon rumbled across the toll bridge and on into Bendición. Here the trip was to be broken. Dan saw Don Martin and Marillita installed at the hotel. He ate his dinner in their company and then, while Martin O'Connor went upon his own business and while Marillita, accompanied by her chaperone, shopped from the meager supplies of Bendición's merchants, Dan strolled down the street to Rand Fitzpatrick's saloon.

Fitzpatrick was not in. Dan stood talking with the bartender while he waited. Presently Fitzpatrick returned.

He shook hands with Dan and led him to a table in the rear of the room. Seated there, their greetings and small talk done, Fitzpatrick asked a question.

"I hear you're goin' to be married. That so?"

"That's so," Dan agreed pleasantly. "In October. Fitz, will you stand up with me?"

Fitzpatrick's face showed his surprise. "Me?"

"You. There's no one I'd rather have."

A slow grin spread across Fitzpatrick's face. "Think of that now," he said. And then: "Of course I will, Dan."

"That's settled then," Dan Shea said. "I'll let you know when, Fitz."

A silence fell between them while Fitzpatrick looked at his fingers, nervously tapping on the table top. "You had any more trouble?" he asked suddenly.

"*I've* had none," Dan answered. "But there's a suit . . ."

"I know about that," Fitzpatrick interrupted.

"We're on the way to Albuquerque now," Dan said. "We'll hire a lawyer and clear the thing up. I wonder why the De la Luzes started it, Fitz. Have you heard anything?"

For a moment Fitzpatrick did not answer, then, leaning a little further and keeping his voice lowered, he said: "It's Delaney, Dan."

"Delaney?" Dan Shea was startled.

Fitzpatrick nodded solemnly. "It's him," he repeated. "He's got hold of Ramon an' some more of the La Luz outfit. He's representing them."

Dan frowned. "But . . ." he began.

"You hear talk around town," Fitzpatrick interposed hastily. "Nothin' very definite, nothin' very much, but you hear talk. They're out to get O'Connor, Dan. They're goin' to get him if they can. Don Martin's rode high. He's done a lot of things. He's a big man. They aim to get him. It ain't just the La Luz outfit an' Delaney; it's a lot more than that."

Dan Shea sat quiet, and Fitzpatrick leaned back. There was a bitter twist on Dan's lips, a sardonic gleam in his blue eyes. They were out to get Martin

O'Connor, not just the La Luz family, not just George Delaney, but the whole countryside. Dan knew how that worked. Let some man rise up, let some man gain power, let him achieve, and all the others of the pack would strive to pull him down. There might be men in Bendición and around the town who would not lift a hand to hurt O'Connor. Neither would they lift a hand to help him. Arrogance has no friends. Power has sycophants but no partisans. Wealth and achievement, position and place, have no sympathizers. There would be many who would delight to see Don Martin O'Connor dragged down. There would be few, if any, who would help to maintain him in his present status. That is human nature, and Dan Shea knew it.

"I'm in this, Fitz," he said gently. "You knew that, didn't you?"

Fitzpatrick's shrug was eloquent. "Knowin' you, I knew that you was in it."

A moment's silence lay between the men, and then Dan spoke again. "Yes, I'm in it. All the way."

CHAPTER NINE:
"IF YOU COME AGAIN
I'LL KILL YOU!"

In Albuquerque the morning after their arrival Dan
Shea and Martin O'Connor sought out Bruno Gotleib. They found the swarthy little lawyer in his
office, and after greetings and introductions had
been exchanged they plunged immediately into
their business. O'Connor told the story, rumbling
out the words, giving vent to anger now and again
as he spoke. Gotleib listened, and when the tale
was done rested a moment in thought. When he
looked up he spoke crisply.

"I'll handle the matter for you," he decided.
"We'll prepare an answer and file it. We may have
to send to Mexico City for the records. This will be
an expensive business, Don Martin."

O'Connor nodded. Gotleib spoke again. "Do you
want me to represent Mr Louder in this suit?"

"Yes," O'Connor answered. "But I'm payin' for
the whole thing."

"Now that you've brought up the matter"—
Gotleib's eyes met O'Connor squarely—"you'd better give me some money for a retaining fee and for
expenses."

"How much?" O'Connor asked.

Gotleib thought a moment. "A thousand dollars," he said.

"I'll get it at the bank," Don Martin announced. "Come with me, Dan."

All three men arose. "I've a little business at the bank," Gotleib said. "I'll go with you."

Taking their hats, the three left the office and walked down to the low brick building which housed the private banking firm of Stern and Harris with whom O'Connor did business. When they entered the bank Stern, the senior partner, came to them and conducted the trio into his private office. Before Don Martin could state his mission Stern began at once to talk.

"We received the drafts for the wool, Mr O'Connor," he announced. "They came in a week ago. I sent you a letter acknowledging their receipt."

"I got it," Don Martin said. "I . . ."

"I've some bad news for you," Stern interposed gravely. "I was served with an attachment on your account yesterday."

"What?" Martin O'Connor half rose from his chair and then sank back once more.

"Your account has been attached," Stern repeated. "I'm sorry, Mr O'Connor."

Martin O'Connor looked blankly first at Nathan Stern and then at Dan and Gotleib. "But what's that for?" he demanded.

Stern shrugged. "I don't know," he answered. "All I know is that your account has been attached. We're forbidden to release any of it."

Anger began to show on Martin O'Connor's face. "You mean I can't have any of my money?" he rasped.

"The account has been attached," Stern repeated nervously. "I'm sorry, but we can't release any of the money until the attachment has been removed."

"Then I'll borrow!" Martin O'Connor announced. "Make out a note for a thousand dollars, Stern. I'll sign it, and you can give me the money."

Stern's face twisted nervously. "I'm sorry . . ." he began.

"You'll not let me have it?" O'Connor glared at the banker. "Is that it? I've done my business with you for years, an' you'll not make me a loan?"

"I'm sorry," Stern said again. "I understand that you're in legal difficulties, Mr O'Connor. The policy of the bank . . ."

"To hell with your bank an' your policy!" Don Martin roared. "Come, men. We'll get out of this nest of cheats!"

With Stern still expostulating, Martin O'Connor jerked on his hat and stamped his way to the door. Dan Shea and Bruno Gotleib, after an exchange of glances, followed him out.

All the way to Gotleib's office Don Martin stalked ahead in silent fury. It was not until they were in the quiet of Gotleib's room that the dam broke. Then Don Martin, unrestrained, loosened his wrath. There was no stopping or staying him. He cursed the bank, its partners, its root and branch, vowing that never again would he do business with Stern and Harris; that he would ruin them; that he would never forgive this indignity. There was nothing to do with Don Martin but to let his wrath run its course. Dan Shea and Gotleib sat and listened.

Dan Shea had shipped his wool with O'Connor. There would be no money from that source available. Yet money was needed and immediately.

O'Connor cursed and raged, but Dan's mind was not on what the older man was saying. Instead, in his mind, a plan began to take form. Presently Martin O'Connor ran down, stopped and, looking from one to the other of his companions, asked a question.

"What are we goin' to do?"

"I'll prepare an answer and file it," Gotleib announced. "As far as I'm concerned, Don Martin, you needn't give me any money. I'll be glad to take care of the work and the fees. But . . ."

"But Mr Gotleib will be at considerable expense," Dan said easily. "It isn't fair to ask him to put his own money in jeopardy." His eyes were on the lawyer as he spoke, and he could see that Gotleib was relieved.

"You've always got to consider," Dan continued, "that we might lose the suit."

Martin O'Connor glared at Dan. "Lose the suit?" he thundered. "We'll not lose it. I'll take it to the highest court in the country! I'll . . ."

"And all that will cost money," Dan interrupted. "I'll tell you, Don Martin: I've some money left. We'll use that."

"Your money?" Martin O'Connor stared at Dan. "But . . ."

"It will do to start." Dan was unbuttoning his shirt and fumbling with the buckle of his money belt. He drew out the belt, placed it on the table and unbuckled a pocket. "There isn't much there," he said, turning to Gotleib, "but, like I say, we can start with that. And Don Martin will have more. He'll have all that you need."

"But my money's in the bank an' I can't get it,"

O'Connor rasped. "The money from the wool an' . . ."

Dan grinned at O'Connor. "There's plenty of sheep on El Puerto del Sol," he said. "And there's a market in Colorado. Don Martin will have enough money, Mr Gotleib."

Martin O'Connor sat down. Gotleib was smiling. "Apparently you haven't much to worry about, Don Martin," the lawyer said.

"Not while I've got Dan to do my thinkin' for me," O'Connor agreed. "I'd of sold my lambs an' wethers. I knew I could do that, but faith, I was so mad I'd forgot about it." He laughed. "Stickin' to your last, Danny," he observed, turning once more to Dan Shea. "You came to me with the idea of trailin' sheep to Colorado an' I wouldn't let you have 'em. I wanted you with me, an' now you've caught me in a crack an' you'll trail the sheep after all. It's a hardheaded, stubborn lad you are."

Dan Shea was smiling. "About five thousand head will do to start with," he said. "Young ewes. I don't think we need to worry about the money, Mr Gotleib."

Gotleib's thin hands stacked papers. "I'll go right ahead and prepare an answer," he announced. "I'll send a man to Santa Fe to search the records and I'll see what I can do about removing this attachment, though I'm afraid that won't be much. Don Martin, will you and your daughter and Mr Shea dine with me tonight? I'd be very pleased."

Martin O'Connor nodded his shaggy head. "Aye," he answered, "we'll dine with you. An' I tell you right now, Gotleib, I'm keepin' Dan Shea in the family. He's goin' to marry Marillita."

* * *

There was some further talk with Bruno Gotleib before Dan and O'Connor were ready to leave the office. Martin O'Connor's anger still smoldered, and once or twice it flared up, particularly when the attachment of his bank account was mentioned. When finally the details were settled and the plan of action outlined and the two men departed, they had covered the ground thoroughly and, too, they had definitely made an appointment to dine with Bruno Gotleib at his home that evening. Walking back to the hotel, Martin O'Connor was silent for most of the distance. Before they reached the hotel, however, he spoke.

"I don't know what I'd do without you, Dan," he said. "You kept me from fightin' Louder. I'd of done that, for the man rubs me the wrong way. You kept me from losin' my head at the bank an' in Gotleib's office. It's a mystery to me how I got along without you before you came."

Dan laughed. "It seems to me that you did all right," he said. "You held El Puerto del Sol together and put the place on its feet before you ever heard of me."

O'Connor shook his head. "I'm gettin' along in years," he announced. "I know just one way to do things an' that's to fight an' bull 'em through. You're smart, Danny, but you'll fight. I've seen you fight."

Dan did not answer. He was staring across the street. Delaney and Ramon de la Luz were walking together on the opposite side, their heads bent as they talked. Dan Shea stopped short and O'Connor took another step, and then he also stopped.

"What is it, Dan?" he asked quickly.

Delaney and Ramon had entered a building and

were lost to sight. Dan controlled the anger that welled up in him, and yet his voice was thick as he answered: "George Delaney, damn him!"

O'Connor—who had seen neither Delaney nor Ramon—stared curiously at his companion. Dan blurted out words. "I've as much reason to be in this as you have. This is as much my job as it is yours. Marillita . . ." He broke off.

"You're lookin' after her, Dan. Is that it?" Still O'Connor eyed his friend.

Dan nodded. He was looking after Marillita. That was part of it, that and his friendship for Martin O'Connor and his own interests as Don Martin's *partidario.* But that was not all. Deep down in Dan Shea was his ingrained hatred for George Delaney. Startled by the thought, he realized that, regardless of Marillita or Don Martin or anything else, he would have entered this fight, entered it for the sole purpose of beating Delaney.

"Let's go to the hotel," he said abruptly.

Marillita was waiting for them in the hotel. She had shopped all morning and was filled with ideas and a desire to show her purchases. While she talked Don Martin smiled fondly at his daughter, but Dan stood silent. The thought that he must destroy this pleasure pained him.

"And I bought curtains," Marillita continued joyously. "Drapes for all the windows and . . . What is the matter, Dan?"

"I'm sorry," Dan said bluntly, "but we can't buy them now, Marillita."

"Of course you can buy them," O'Connor boomed. "There's nothin' to keep you from . . ."

"Not now," Dan interrupted firmly. "Not until I come back from Colorado."

"From Colorado?" Marillita spoke her surprise. "But . . ."

"There's no need to go into it," O'Connor said hastily.

Dan Shea shook his head. Martin O'Connor had kept details from his daughter, had shielded Marillita. Not so Dan Shea. He knew the stuff of which the girl was made, and to him his marriage would be a partnership. What he faced, what Martin O'Connor faced, Marillita must also face.

"I'll tell you," he said brusquely. "I'll have to go to Colorado." He continued then, telling Marillita about the things that had happened during the morning, detailing the difficulties that confronted Martin O'Connor and El Puerto del Sol, outlining the plans that had been made, going over it all despite Martin O'Connor's frown of disapproval.

"So you see," Dan concluded, "that we can't buy things now, Marillita, and that I've got to go to Colorado with the sheep. You see that, don't you?"

The girl was slow in answering. She stood with lowered eyes staring at the floor. When she lifted her head there was a smile for Dan Shea. "Of course I see," she announced. "I'll go to the stores this afternoon and take back the things I've bought. It's all right, Dan. I'm glad you told me. You had to tell me."

Dan glanced at Martin O'Connor and then turned to the girl. "Of course I had to," he agreed.

That night the three, Don Martin, Marillita and Dan Shea, dined with Bruno Gotleib. Gotleib's wife, a small, gracious woman, was a perfect hostess, and at the table there was no mention made of the errand that had brought the guests from El Puerto del

Sol. It was late when the group left Gotleib's house and, in the lawyer's carriage, was driven back to the hotel.

Don Martin and Marillita went to their rooms to rest. In the morning the party would leave for their return journey. Dan Shea, lingering in the lobby, paid for their accommodations and then, smoking a cigar, walked out to the porch and stood thinking, letting the cool breeze whip away the smoke.

It was odd, he thought, how he should have come to be the controlling influence in all these happenings. He had come into the country without particular destination in mind. His sole idea had been to recoup the losses he had suffered in the North. Now here he was, in partnership with Martin O'Connor, engaged to marry the most desirable woman in the world and embroiled in a fight. Had it been through chance, he wondered? Had all this happened through circumstance, or was there some guiding spirit that had ordered his life, that had brought him to New Mexico Territory, sent him to Martin O'Connor's door and placed Marillita in his arms? Dan Shea looked up at the stars and wondered.

As he stood there, the cigar finished and thrown away, still musing, still pondering the events, still questioning himself concerning them, he was aroused from his introspection by a swift step on the porch. Dan turned. Light from the lobby streamed through a window, and Ramon de la Luz crossed that light. Dan faced the man in the shadows, and De la Luz stopped.

"Señor Shea?" he asked.

"I'm Dan Shea."

Ramon de la Luz continued, speaking in Spanish. "You came with Martin O'Connor?"

"Yes."

"I came to warn you," De la Luz announced. "Leave El Puerto del Sol. Leave Señor O'Connor. This business does not concern. If you value your life you will leave it alone."

With an effort Dan Shea restrained himself. His mind cried to him for action; his muscles ached with their tension. "George Delaney sent you," Dan Shea said sternly. "Go back to him and tell him that you've failed."

"There are a great many of us," Ramon de la Luz said softly. "You have already made enemies, señor. I am giving you a chance. You . . ."

Dan Shea's restraint broke. His left hand, powerful as a vise, shot out and caught the coat of Ramon de la Luz. Dan pulled the man toward him, nearly lifting De la Luz from his feet, holding him tightly so that in the darkness of the porch their faces almost touched.

"Get out!" Dan Shea rasped thickly, his hand trembling with his wrath. "Get out, *cabrón!*"

He thrust forward then, releasing his hold. Ramon de la Luz reeled across the streaming light from the window, brought up against the wall and, staggering, recovered his balance. Dan, controlling his anger, holding himself as best he could, spoke once more, made one more statement.

"If you come to me again, you or Delaney, I'll kill you! Get out!"

CHAPTER TEN:
TRAIL NORTH

On the night of his first day out from El Puerto del Sol Dan Shea sat beside his campfire and looked into the darkness where his sheep were bedded. Out there in the dark beyond the firelight there were five thousand head of El Puerto del Sol ewes. About him, clustered close, were his herders: Hilario Bargas, Nopomencenco Montano with the knife scar across his face; Hipolito, Nopomencenco's brother; Hilario's two sons, Eusabio and Cercencio, strong as young oxen; Juan Vigil, quarter-breed Comanche, and Vicente Lebya, the Apache boy. Seven men in all, hardy, strong-bodied, loyal to Dan Shea and to El Puerto del Sol. They were quiet, respecting the silence of their *patrón,* and close beside them their sheep dogs lay, eyes half shut against the firelight.

It was odd, Dan Shea reflected, sitting there in the firelight, how he should have come to be here with the sheep; odd and yet natural too. How could he have done otherwise? he asked himself. All the past events marched before him. His arrival in Bendición, his encounter with Martin O'Connor, his partnership, his love for Marillita, each fell into ordered sequence. Dan Shea shifted position beside the crackling fire, and his thoughts went on.

Marillita's parting kiss was still warm upon Dan's lips as he sat there musing. It would remain, warm and promising, all through his long journey, he knew, just as would Don Martin's parting hand-shake remain, strong and reassuring. Dan's eyes lighted as he thought of Marillita and Don Martin, then they dulled again. There were things to think of other than the sweet bitterness of parting. Many things.

This was his task, this business of trailing five thousand sheep north to a Colorado market. This task he had set himself for the benefit of them all, for the welfare of El Puerto del Sol. But he wished that it had not been necessary. Others had wished that too: Marillita and Don Martin and Jesse Louder. Dan remembered his talk with Louder, the half suspicion, half frankness of the man. Dan lifted his hand and rubbed his forehead as he re-called that meeting.

Louder, his hostility apparent, had come to him as Dan prepared for his journey. There had been difficulties between Louder and O'Connor, and now this suit had revived all the old dissension. Louder spoke of them frankly.

"I wish you were goin' to be here, Shea," he had concluded their conversation. "You an' me get along. I don't get along so good with O'Connor."

"I wish I didn't have to go," Dan Shea had an-swered. "I couldn't think of anything else to do though."

"No," Louder said moodily. "I guess there wasn't anything else to do."

"And I'll be back," Dan promised. "Mr Louder,

like you've said, you and me get along. I'm going to ask you to be patient while I'm gone. If anything comes up I ask you to wait until I'm back before you do anything about it. Will you do that?"

Louder thought for a time and then nodded. "That's fair enough, I guess," he said. "I won't make any promises, Shea, but I won't go off half cocked."

"That's all I ask," Dan Shea said.

Louder was silent again and then thrust out his hand. "So long, Shea," he said. "I'll push on home." Again he hesitated. Then: "I guess things will be about the same when you get back."

There beside his campfire Dan Shea smiled. Jesse Louder had made no promises, but his handshake and parting words had been enough. Dan had an ally in Louder.

The smile faded and Dan's eyes grew bleak. There were others besides Louder in Bendición and the adjoining countryside who were not allies. Of these, George Delaney was pre-eminent. Thoughtfully Dan considered Delaney and his part in all these happenings. Delaney gave them point, had surely been the motivating force. Perhaps Delaney was simply shrewd. Dan could not believe that. He could not believe that it was opportunism that had brought Delaney into this affair, that had made George Delaney the representative for Ramon de la Luz in the suit. No, knowing Delaney as he did, Dan was sure that suit and claim, trouble and grief, all the difficulties that had descended upon El Puerto del Sol, originated in Delaney's fertile mind. Dan scowled at the thought.

"Coffee, Señor Dan?" Eusabio spoke softly beside Dan Shea. With a start Dan was brought back to the present. He reached out his hand, and the scowl was erased by a smile.

"Gracias, Eusabio," Dan Shea said gratefully.

In the morning the herd went on, dirty gray against the brown of the good fall grass, stretching out, changing shape but moving north as the ewes grazed. Behind the ewes and about them the herders and their dogs held place, watching wanderers, preventing straying, always moving forward. Back of the herd came Eusabio, the cook with his burros and the camp equipment. Ahead of the herd Dan Shea rode, scouting the country, choosing the course, selecting the camp site when night came. Three hundred miles to the north lay Colorado and the market. Slowly the sheep moved northward.

Day dawdled into day, each like its fellow. Fall rains came, cold and cutting to the skin as wind-driven drops swept earthward. Sunshine succeeded the rain, and Eusabio dried the scanty bedding. Some few sheep, finding whorled milkweed, ate it and died. The mornings and the evenings merged into one until the days had no identity, and ever the herd crept slowly on.

Then on a bright morning, riding ahead of the herd, Dan saw smoke on the eastern horizon. Rising beneath the morning haze, the smoke intrigued Dan as he watched. He spoke briefly to Eusabio and, turning his mule, rode toward the east, leaving the herd to Hilario's watchfulness.

After an hour of riding Dan was tempted to turn back. The smoke had died into a threadlike column and then was gone. Dan debated momentarily and then, deciding to top one last rise, rode on again. Reaching the summit of the slope, he looked down into the valley below. There, before him, lay the source of the smoke. For a full five minutes Dan sat there, sickened but not so sickened as to be unwary. Then with his heels he urged the mule forward and rode down.

There was not much left in the valley. The little plaza was a cluster of smoke-blackened rock squares, the dirt roofs fallen into the ruins or sagging over them. Where hay had been stacked there was black ash, some of it still smoldering. A wagon was charred wood with its irons still hot to the touch. Destruction was all about, and the scent of smoke was tinged with the odor of burned flesh.

Dan Shea, his rifle across his arm, left the mule and walked gingerly among the ruins. Here he found a body, the scalp ripped from the head, flies buzzing about, already at work. Here a woman had died, the mouth of the corpse still open in a soundless scream. Here a man had fought. The arrow in his throat had killed him. Dan Shea whirled about, the big Sharps leaping to his shoulder, his finger on the trigger. He poised, ready, and the sound that had alarmed him was repeated, the rasp of movement on stone. Then timidly a voice said: "Señor Shea . . ."

Dan lowered the weapon. "Vicente!" he said sternly. "¡Ven acá!"

Vicente, eyes downcast, came from behind a ruined house. He said no word but advanced, coming like a dog would come to an angry master, obedient and placating, but afraid.

"What are you doing here?" Dan Shea demanded.

"I followed you," Vicente answered. "Always I follow you. Every day."

There, amidst that desolation, with death and ruin all about, Dan Shea almost laughed. Here then was explained the silence of Vicente when Dan spoke to him concerning the happenings in camp. Here, too, was explained a certain taciturnity among the herders. By mutual consent and agreement between them they had chosen to keep a watch over Dan Shea. Vicente was that watch. Now Dan knew why, when upon occasion he had returned to camp and found Vicente missing, Eusabio had spoken concerning some errand that occupied the boy. Now Dan knew why Hilario's hostility toward Vicente had decreased until it was no more. Vicente was carrying a Springfield across his arm, and there was a knife at his belt, and he limped.

"I hurt my leg," Vicente said apologetically. "My foot slipped on a stone; otherwise the señor would not have heard me."

Dan eyed him sternly. "You follow me every day?" he demanded.

"*Sí . . .*" Vicente's voice was resigned. "*Yo creí . . .* I believed . . ." He broke off and made hasty amendment: "*Nosotros creímos . . .* we thought . . ."

"That I was a child that must be watched?" Dan finished, his voice harsh.

"No, señor. But you ride out alone, and we knew that was not good. We would not have you hurt, señor. What would we do without you?"

"And so you followed?" Dan Shea said. "I think . . . well, no matter. Later we will talk of that. Now: Who was here? Who did this?"

Vicente straightened, and his eyes swept over the ruins, over the blackened stone of the houses, the still-smoldering hay, the burned wagon, the silently screaming woman and the man with the arrow in his throat. Black and beady and inscrutable, the eyes returned to Dan Shea's face.

"Los indios de la Sierra Blanca," Vicente answered gutturally. "Apaches."

CHAPTER ELEVEN:
SURPRISE ATTACK

There was nothing that could be done at the *placita*. With Vicente walking beside the mule, Dan Shea started back toward the west. Just at the edge of the ruins Vicente stopped and lifted his hand. Dan halted the mule. Vicente was listening intently. He turned toward a shed, the posts burned away and the roof sagging, listened a moment more and then went swiftly to the wreckage. When Vicente emerged his face was triumphant, and he held out a small bundle of inert fur. Dan Shea looked at the trophy. Vicente had found a puppy, so small that its eyes were not yet opened. The pup hung down from Vicente's hand. In all that desolation only the one small spark of life remained. With Vicente carrying the dog and trotting beside Dan's mule, the two went back toward the sheep.

The ewes were spread out and grazing peacefully. Men assembled about Dan Shea and Vicente, listening to the tale that was told them, alarm in their eyes as they heard of the rape of the *placita*. Bold men these herders, else they had not ventured on this journey; fighters, ready with knife or gun, but with a tradition behind them: the tradition of fear of the Apache.

Dan Shea watched their eyes and saw their fear. He spoke brusquely. The Apaches had gone on. There was no cause for worry. Even Apaches would hesitate to attack so strong a party as this. Despite Dan's assurances fear lingered in the eyes of his men. Dan Shea took counsel with himself.

In company with all his kind he cherished one idea: Dead Indians were good Indians. Frontier experience lay behind Dan Shea. The Apaches, he believed, would hardly overlook this flock moving through the country. The sheep themselves would be of little value to a raiding party; the ewes were too slow of movement to be stolen and driven. Horses and cattle were more to the savage fancy. Still there was loot in the packs and scalps on the heads of the herders, both desirable from the Apache viewpoint. That little raiding party was a menace.

Dan knew his men. Experienced in fighting, he realized that under the strain of waiting for an attack, in the surprise of an attack, these men might break. If that occurred sheep and men were lost.

But there was an alternative. They need not wait, need not sit helplessly, anticipating an attack. They themselves were in the position of initiative, and under certain circumstances the herders would be brave enough. Dan rubbed his bearded jaw and looked at his men and reached a decision. Calling Nopomencenco and Vicente to him, he gave instructions. They were, Dan ordered, to scout the country about the herd and make sure that it was clear of Apaches.

Nopomencenco and Vicente departed. Dan ordered Eusabio to prepare food, forbidding the kindling of a fire. Hilario he sent to the ridge north of the little valley wherein the flock grazed. Hilario was an outpost.

The men munched cold food and eyed Dan Shea. They believed in him, would follow him blindly and loyally. On Dan's shoulders rested the responsibility, upon him the command. The sun was straight above. It was noon. Dan sent Cercencio to replace Hilario at the outpost.

Time wore on. The sheep grazed peacefully. Without orders the herders held them in the valley, men and dogs turning back those venturesome ewes that sought to climb the ridges. Eusabio concerned himself with the puppy rescued from the *placita.* There was a goat in the herd, a doe that was followed by a three-months-old kid. Eusabio caught the doe and brought her in. He tied the goat's feet and, bringing the pup to her, placed the small dog adjacent to her udder. The goat fought and struggled and finally, giving up, lay still and watched her captor with wicked, black-slotted, yellow eyes. Dan, strolling over, stood beside Eusabio. The pup sucked a teat, with small whimpering noises when he lost it.

Eusabio sought relief from the tension in talk. This, he informed Dan, was the way to raise a sheep dog. A dog, taken from its mother before its eyes opened and given a goat to nurse, grew up with the idea that it was not a dog but a goat. So later the dog would consort with the goats and with the sheep, retaining its natural antagonism against coyotes and wolves, but always believing that it was a goat. Dan nodded. He had heard the tale before. Perhaps it was true, perhaps not. At any rate, dogs that were so raised made good sheep dogs, working intelligently and quietly with their charges.

Among the grouped herders Hilario spoke sharply and pointed. Dan Shea, following the direction of that pointing arm, saw a man coming down from the north, trotting along, a small black dot against the green grass. The man came on, resolved into Nopomencenco, drew close, reached Dan Shea and stopped.

Nopomencenco was panting. He drew great breaths into his deep chest and let them go. Dan waited. Still short of breath, Nopomencenco reported. They had, he said, found the Apaches. There were tracks to the north. The Apaches had seen the herd; of that Nopomencenco was certain. But the Indians were waiting. Perhaps five miles north they were. Vicente had located them.

"Where is Vicente?" Dan demanded.

He was watching the Apaches, Nopomencenco told him. There were not many in the raiding party. Vicente had sent him, Nopomencenco, back to report to Señor Shea.

"How many Apaches?" Dan asked.

Nopomencenco shrugged. He was not sure. Perhaps a dozen, perhaps a few more. Nopomencenco waited, watching his *patrón*. So, too, waited the others. Dan rubbed his hand against the stubble on his cheek, eyed his men and then spoke.

"We'll go to them," he directed, smiling grimly. "They are waiting for us. It would be bad to disappoint them." A grin broke on Hilario's bearded face. All about Dan Shea the tension broke. It was almost as though he had invited these men to a fiesta. They would wait no longer. Here was opportunity to avenge themselves upon a hereditary enemy. There was a sudden babble of talk which Dan sternly checked.

He spoke rapidly. Cercencio would remain with the sheep. He could, with the help of the dogs, hold them in the valley. The rest were to accompany Dan Shea. They must obey his orders absolutely.

From about Dan the voices came in agreement. Dan stooped and picked up the Sharps.

The men followed Dan out of the valley. Cercencio, resolute and with a Springfield across his knees, remained in a cluster of rocks. If they did not return Cercencio was to go back. He was to abandon the sheep and return to El Puerto del Sol with the word, so ran Dan's instructions. But they would return, he reassured Cercencio, talking to him in private. There was nothing to fear. Cercencio nodded. He understood.

Each man that followed Dan Shea carried a rifle and ammunition. Each man, too, had a knife. As to other personal armament Dan did not know. He himself dangled the heavy Sharps from his hand, and under his arm, beneath his coat already becoming ragged, there was his Colt. Nopomencenco walked beside Dan, a guide and pathfinder. So, on foot and cautiously, they traveled north.

Beyond the ridge north of the valley that contained the herd the country fell away in long folds. There were wide draws that ran across the line of march. Nopomencenco, questioned by Dan, spoke briefly concerning the nature of the country. For the most part, the herder informed, the ridges and their concomitant hollows ran east and west. There was one long arroyo that swung in a slanting circle toward the river to the west. Dan nodded. So much he could see. If there was water it would be in the arroyo. If there was water the Apaches would wait beside it. While the others waited Dan made his plan. Where, he asked Nopomencenco, had he left Vicente? Nopomencenco pointed and explained, and Dan listened.

He knew—or believed he knew—the operation of the Apache mind. The Apache was like a snake. He hunted when necessary but, by choice, the Apache waited beside a trail for his game to come to him. So might these be doing. If the raiding party knew of the presence of the herd, and Nopomencenco was sure that they did, then logically the savages would be considering the idea of attack, of loot and pleasure. They favored early morning or late evening for their raids. At those times men are unsuspecting and relaxed. And the Apaches had no reason to believe that the men with the sheep knew of their presence. Dan frowned. If he knew surely where the Apaches waited he would be able to beat them to the surprise. But he had no certain knowledge. Perhaps if he followed up the arroyo, scouting ahead with Nopomencenco . . .

"Allá está Vicente," Nopomencenco announced.

Dan searched the country below him. He could see nothing until his swarthy companion pointed. Then close by the arroyo he sighted movement. A man—at least Dan believed it to be a man— appeared momentarily between two clumps of mesquite.

"Es Vicente!" Nopomencenco said positively.

That might be true. At least the arroyo was the logical place to reach. Dan nodded and started down the slope, his companions following.

There were other ridges between that first high vantage point and the arroyo. They lost sight of the dry stream bed; then, crowning a rise, they sighted it again, much closer now. The herders remained behind the protection of the low ridge, and Dan and Nopomencenco crawled ahead. The bank of the arroyo, two hundred yards away, lay barren of all life. Dan glanced at Nopomencenco doubtfully, turned his head again to look at the arroyo, and his eyes widened with surprise. Vicente was walking from the arroyo toward them, his rifle swinging nonchalantly from his hand, pride evinced in his every step. Dan lifted his head, twisted his body and, seated, waited for Vicente's arrival.

Vicente was both boastful and scornful. He had marked the progress of Dan Shea and the herders across every ridge, he said. Dan doubted this. They were a full four miles and more than an hour's travel from the sheep. No man, Dan believed, could see so far. He did not voice his doubts aloud. Vicente continued. The Apaches were in the arroyo. They had camped beside water. They were sheep, Vicente boasted; White Mountain Apaches, not at all like the Chiricahuas from whom Vicente came. Now they were moving, coming down the arroyo.

"How many?" Dan demanded curtly.

Vicente held up both hands, the fingers spread, then he closed one fist and left three fingers extended on the other hand. Thirteen.

Dan nodded. His eyes scanned the bank of the arroyo. He stood up and gestured. Behind him his men arose. Swiftly Dan led the way across the expanse from ridge to arroyo bank. There, where mesquite grew, he stopped. The herders eyed the mesquite doubtfully. They knew its toughness, knew its sharp thorns. Still, at low-voiced command, they wormed their way into the thorny thickets, each man choosing a place, each man selecting shelter. They could tolerate the scratching and cuts of the thorn; they could bear with the sand and the waiting and the discomfort, for they were being given a chance to beat the Apache at his own game of ambush and throat cutting. To each man Dan Shea spoke his warning. They must wait until he fired the first shot; they must lie quiet and concealed. If they did not the Apaches would be at their throats.

In his own place of concealment, flanked by Vicente and Nopomencenco, Dan sprawled down. Mesquite roots dug at him. A thorny branch trailed across his neck so that when he moved ever so slightly the thorns pricked cruelly. His Sharps was shoved out, and before him was the thin screen of mesquite through which he could see the arroyo. All along, on either side, Dan Shea's companions waited, lying in ambush, the success of all dependent upon the quietness and fortitude of each individual. Dan watched the arroyo.

Time dragged by interminably. A big red ant, exploring, found Dan's arm and bit viciously, the sting almost unbearable. By shifting his eyes Dan could see Vicente's head some eight feet to his left, the black hair bound with an old rag. The head lifted. Dan's eyes were on the arroyo again. To the right, up the arroyo, a savage appeared riding a gaunt pony, moccasined legs dangling, a rifle resting across his thighs as he rode.

The single savage came on, passed by Dan Shea, passed by Vicente. Not sixty yards away he was following the course of the dry stream. Dan let him go. To the right Nopomencenco sighed faintly, the barest whisper of sound. Dan did not move. The Apache rode on.

Now others appeared, a straggling line of them,

two grouped together, then three, then one, then the others. The leader passed by Dan Shea. Dan counted. There were twelve in view. Dan held his finger on the trigger of the Sharps, cocked the hammer and took careful aim. When the Sharps roared the whole thicket of mesquite responded, leaping into life with the crash of the rifles.

Dan came up to his feet. Legs widespread, another shell sliding into the greasy, smoking breech of the Sharps, he turned to the left. There, up the arroyo, that first Apache—the scout who had passed by, was bent low over his pony's neck, and sand was churning beneath the pony's neck, and sand was churning beneath the pony's feet. Again the Sharps steadied and then spilled its contents. The heavy five-hundred-grain slug must have pierced man and horse, for both went down. Dan swung back to the right again.

There was wild confusion in the arroyo. From both arroyo and mesquite the yells arose. A savage, wiry and swift as a cat, scrambled up the opposite bank, poised for a moment and then collapsed into a bundle of rags and brown flesh. From the mesquite, heedless of thorns or footing, the herders came leaping, whooping, savage as the Apaches themselves. Dan Shea dropped the Sharps and with his pistol in hand crashed through the growth and ran to the arroyo.

For perhaps a minute the fight raged and then, sudden as it had begun, was done. The herders, Nopomencenco and Hilario, Eusabio and Vicente, all of them, stood panting, the fierceness draining away from them, remaining only in their eyes and distorted faces, and in the arroyo, against its banks and on its sand, the Apaches lay, twisted and grotesque, caught and destroyed in just such a trap as they themselves delighted in setting.

There was, of course, an aftermath to the fight. The herders and Dan Shea moved about the scene of the fighting, examining the bodies and searching them. From the evidence they collected there was no doubt that these were the marauders who had looted the *placita.* One savage corpse bore a gold cross about its neck; another wore earrings, and there were remnants of garments and fresh scalps to show.

Contrary to their general custom, the raiders had not traveled lightly laden. There were two pack horses down in the arroyo, killed perhaps in the first volley. The packs of these were opened and examined by the herders, and from them such articles as caught the fancy were removed. In this Dan Shea played no part. He stood watching and, as the shadows grew long in the arroyo, called his men off from their pursuit. The hour was late and night was coming. They must hurry back to the waiting sheep. Dan gave his orders. So, filled with their success, drunk with it, laden with the weapons, the savage finery, the loot that they had taken from the looters, Dan Shea and his men started back, retracing their journey toward the herd.

It was dusk when they reached the valley. Cercencio arose stiffly from amidst his rock fort and welcomed them. The herd was intact. There had been no alarm, Cercencio said, but he had heard the firing to the north. The men, weary, went about their appointed duties. A fire was built. Eusabio prepared food. The men ate. Then with the firelight flickering, with the tenseness eased, they rested, each man recounting his own exploits, so concerned with his own valor and glory that he hardly listened to the tales of his neighbors.

Dan Shea sat watching them, smiling a little. These men were children, strong in body, simple in mind. As he listened to the talk his smile broadened. A man without knowledge listening to the talk might well believe that these few men had met and vanquished the Apache nation. They were scratched with thorns, and more than one of them bore signs of the conflict, cuts received when they charged in to finish the fight. Their clothing was torn, more ragged than it had been before the battle. They were weary, but the excitement of their recollections buoyed them. Like children they talked and laughed and glorified themselves and each other.

Close to the fire Vicente bent above a bundle taken from an Apache pack horse. He untied the rawhide thong and laid the bundle open. Dan Shea, rising, strode across to survey Vicente's loot. Vicente looked up and grinned, then, turning his attention to the contents of the pack, spread it out.

There were a few skins, poor things, unworthy of a second glance. There was a pouch which, opened and shaken, gave forth a miscellany of objects: the dried foot of an eagle, the teeth of a wolf, lion claws, small chunks of ocher and white earth and tobacco. A medicine pouch, Dan surmised. There was a long roll wrapped in a sheepskin from which the wool had been removed; there was a coat, small when Vicente held it up for inspection, wrinkled, and still with a sort of dapperness about it. Dan Shea frowned when he saw the coat. It was such a garment as no native would wear. The coat had belonged to a white man. There was confirmatory evidence to that. The last article in the pack was the remains of a derby hat. Crushed and battered though it was, the identity was unmistakable. Dan Shea held out his hand and Vicente placed the hat in it.

Squatting beside the Apache boy, Dan looked at the hat. It was made of hard brown felt and the crown was broken. He turned it in his hand. The leather sweatband was still intact and, faint upon the leather, letters had been stamped, unreadable now, but undoubtedly the initials of the man who had originally purchased the derby. Dan sought further to locate the maker's stamp and, perhaps, the name of the store from which the hat had been purchased. These were too faint for deciphering. He returned the hat to Vicente.

Vicente had opened the roll of sheepskin. Parchments were disclosed. Wordlessly he extended these to Dan Shea. Dan glanced at them and shrugged. He could speak Spanish but he could not read or write the language. These parchments that Vicente held out were written in Spanish and were yellow with age.

"We will take these with us," Dan decided. In his mind was an idea. Perhaps the papers from the sheepskin roll would disclose the identity of the man who had owned the coat and the derby. When he reached a place where there was someone who could read Spanish Dan would make inquiry.

"Save them," he ordered. "I think . . ."

"Señor! Señor Dan!" Eusabio called from across the fire. Dan got up. Eusabio's voice was excited. "Ven acá."

Dan walked around the fire. Eusabio was pointing down and Dan, looking at the place Eusabio indicated, saw that the pup was nursing at the goat's udder. "He has his eyes open!" Eusabio exclaimed. *"Mira, mira,* Señor Dan!"

Dan bent down. It was just as Eusabio had said. The puppy's eyes were open, and when Dan Shea attempted to detach the little dog from the teat the pup clung fiercely and even growled, a bass rumble from the tiny throat.

"Es un bravo," Eusabio exclaimed.

"Bravo," Dan Shea agreed. "That's his name: Bravo!"

Chapter Twelve:
Journey's End

On the evening of the second day following the fight with the Apaches visitors came to Dan Shea's camp. The sheep were bedded on a slope and supper was ready when from a watcher at the herd there came a long yell. Dan Shea, looking up the slope, saw a column of horsemen topping the rise and knew them for what they were: cavalry.

The little troop came on steadily, passed the flock and, halting at command, the troopers lounged in their saddles while the officer and a blue-jeaned guide approached the camp. Dan walked out to meet them.

The officer was Lieutenant Shirby, very young and very eager. The guide, a grizzled oldster, loafed on his horse and chewed tobacco while the lieutenant questioned Dan.

Shirby was on scout. With twenty troopers he was searching for a party of Apaches who had left the Mescalero reservation and gone west. He asked questions and Dan, without definite prevarication, managed to convey the impression that he had not seen Shirby's quarry. Following the brief conversation with Dan Shea, Shirby returned to his men and gave orders. The troopers made camp some two hundred yards away from Dan's fire, and Dan, returning to his own camp, ordered that Hilario butcher two sheep for the soldiers.

Shirby came to thank Dan for the gift and remained to talk. When he had returned through the darkness to his own camp and quiet had fallen on the little valley where the camps were made, Dan sat beside his fire, musing. A soft step broke into his introspection and, looking up, Dan saw the blue-jeaned guide, Landcaster, move into the firelight. Without invitation Landcaster sat down, removed his chew from his mouth and tossed it carelessly into the blaze.

"Where'd you find 'em?" Landcaster drawled.

Dan was startled. "Find who?" he answered.

"Lucero an' his outfit," Landcaster replied easily. "Look. I ain't goin' to say nothin' to the lieutenant. What he don't know won't hurt him. He's pretty young an' he might make some trouble for you because he's all filled up with this 'wards of the guvamint' business. But I seen a pair of moccasins that one of yore men's wearin', an' there's another that's got a beaded pouch that I seen on an Apache buck not three weeks ago. I ain't blind an' I don't figure that yore men traded for them things. What happened?"

There was no use in trying to evade the scout's questions. Dan knew it and, nodding thoughtfully, answered him truthfully. "We ran into them day before yesterday. They'd raided a little place over east of here, an' I saw the smoke. I rode over to see what it was all about and found out what had happened."

Landcaster grunted. "So?" he prompted.

"So we scouted and found 'em," Dan reported

succinctly. "I've got a Chiricahua boy along that thinks I'm a pretty good hombre, and he located them for us. They'd seen us, so we beat them to the jump."

A quizzical grin formed on Landcaster's lips. "Git 'em all?" he drawled.

"Thirteen," Dan answered. "In a big arroyo about ten or twelve miles south of here. They were followin' the arroyo."

Landcaster nodded. "I don't see no particular reason for me to take Shirby there," he said. "Likely he'd want to know what killed 'em, an' I couldn't just put it down to lightnin'. I'll take him over along the river an' let him get some exercise. It'll do him good." He grinned at Dan as one understanding friend to another. For a time the old scout sat staring into the dying embers of the fire, then suddenly he spoke. "Lucero was a half-breed an' plumb bad. He'd worked for white men just long enough to get smart. I knowed there'd be trouble when he come back to the reservation last spring."

The name "Lucero" aroused a responsive chord in Dan's memory. He searched his memory, trying to connect the name with some event and, failing, looked at Landcaster again. "Well?" he prompted.

Landcaster uncoiled his great length and lumbered to his feet. "Well," he drawled, "you saved me a lot of work an' likely some soldier boy's scalp. I'm goin' to bed. Good night, Shea."

"Good night," Dan answered.

The scout disappeared into the darkness.

The soldiers left the following morning, riding on toward the west. Dan watched them go, saw Land-caster turn to wave farewell and lifted his arm in reply. Then as the little line of troopers disappeared he turned to his herd.

Day slid into day once more, blending into a whole. No march was very long; no march was very difficult. Dan Shea, his herders and his sheep, whittled at distance, and then with fall come upon him Dan Shea and his herd came abreast of Albuquerque. Dan left the flock and, taking Eusabio and two burros to pack supplies, rode to the town.

While Eusabio made necessary purchases, Dan interviewed Gotlieb. Gotlieb had news and mail for Dan. There had been trouble in Bendición, the little lawyer informed, and worry showed in his words. Martin O'Connor and Ramon de la Luz had met upon the street and there had been an altercation. Only quick intervention had prevented a killing, for both Ramon and Don Martin had been armed. Too, Gotlieb had no encouraging word concerning the search for the title of El Puerto del Sol. He consulted with Dan, giving what information he had and asking advice. All that Dan could counsel was that the search be continued.

At the lawyer's office Dan read his letters, a note from Don Martin, a brief scrawl from Fitzpatrick and a long letter from Marillita. Don Martin's note showed that he was worried. Fitzpatrick's letter told of the meeting between O'Connor and Ramon de la Luz, and in it Fitzpatrick again assured Dan that he was watching things in Bendición. It was over Marillita's letter that Dan spent time, reading and rereading its passages, warmed and strengthened by the love of the girl. Finished with his mail, he answered it and when he had written to Don Martin, to Fitzpatrick and to Marillita, he gave the letters to Gotleib to post.

"I wish you'd go down there and talk to Don Martin," Dan told Gotleib. "Cheer him up. Make him think that things are coming along all right. He's worried and he's anxious and he might do something that would upset the whole thing. I wish you'd go and visit him."

Gotleib nodded. "I'll go down," he promised, "just as soon as I can. I wish that you hadn't had to leave."

"That's what I wish," Dan answered shortly. "But I did have to."

"Couldn't you sell the sheep here and go back?" Gotleib ventured.

Dan shook his head. "There's no market for sheep here," he said. "And, besides, Delaney and Ramon de la Luz might tie up the sale. I'd better go on."

Dan's words were true. Reluctantly Gotleib agreed and Dan, bidding the lawyer good-by, left the office and went to the supply house where Eusabio had purchased the necessities for the crew. It was midnight before Dan Shea and his cook reached the camp. Eusabio, with the burros unpacked, went to bed and to sleep, but Dan Shea—huddled in his coat, for the night was cold—sat beside the dead fire and stared off into the darkness. He was worried. The news he had was not reassuring, but more than worry possessed him. Sitting there, the bedded sheep a gray mass out in the night, Dan Shea was filled with longing for the soft lips and warm arms of Marillita. It was a bad night, and Dan was glad when dawn streaked the east and the Sandias loomed black and the camp aroused.

From Albuquerque the herd marched north, up

that sheer mesa front called La Bajada, on and on, turning toward the west into the high country. And ever as they moved the days grew shorter and the nights lengthened and the weather became more threatening.

At Arroyo Hondo, above Taos, they crossed the Rio Grande, the hoofs of the ewes drumming on the bridge, and Dan haggling with the bridgekeeper over the toll that he must pay. Beyond the bridge the flock climbed out of the black-lipped canyon of the Rio and out upon the sage-covered, wind-swept plain once more. It was west of the Rio Grande that the storm struck them.

Day dawned, gray and formidable. By midmorning a piercing west wind swept across the sage and snow spat down viciously. The sheep, despite the efforts of the herders, turned tail to the wind and snow and drifted. Inexorable as a rising tide, the herd worked back toward the river, back toward the deep canyon with its sheer rock walls. There was no turning the flock, no handling them. By noon, all thought of food forgotten, the men could not see each other across the drifting herd. Snow rimed the backs of the sheep, turning them from gray to white. The men were white-plastered ghosts moving through the snow. Dan Shea, fighting the drifting sheep, fighting the growing panic of his herders, strove to keep the herd intact and, minute by minute, the snow deepened underfoot and thickened the air.

The canyon was the danger. If the herd struck the rim the leaders would hold back and strive to turn, but under the pressure of their sisters behind the leaders must give way. Then they would go over the rim and down that sheer descent to plunge

to death on the rocks below, first the leaders, then
the followers until only a scant remnant remained
on top. That was the picture; that the danger.
Somehow, in some manner, Dan Shea must avoid
it. He shouted to Hilario, the man nearest him, bidding him stay with the sheep, bidding him hold the
other herders with the herd, and when Hilario's
inarticulate shout came back, whipped by the wind,
Dan Shea left his flock and plunged into the storm,
striking east.

Within a hundred yards the herd was lost. When
he looked back he could not see for the blinding
snow. Dan tried that once and then turned his back
to the storm and forged ahead. He was riding a
mule, a tough, wiry little Spanish "mula" which
carried him directly downwind.

Two miles they went, Dan estimated, and then
the mule hesitated and presently stopped abruptly.
Dan urged his mount ahead, but the mule refused.
Perforce he climbed down, stiffly because of the
cold and his heavy clothing and, leading the mule,
took three more steps. Then he stopped short. Beneath his feet was the black-lipped canyon edge,
and below him, a thousand feet perhaps, the Rio
Grande ran. To Dan's left was a piñon, a single tree
perched precariously amid the rocks. It was a
marker. Tethering the mule to the piñon, Dan explored the rim on foot.

First he went north, searching in vain for the
thing he must have. Time was short. Dan turned
back. The mule marked the piñon and Dan passed
her by. Now he went south, continuing his search,
and within three hundred yards found the thing
he sought. Here a narrow crevasse cut the lip of
the canyon and led down. Dan explored it hastily.

He could not follow out the entire length of the little canyon. There was not time. But it was a slope, however rocky and steep, and as a slope, better than the sheer drop over the rim. Dan went down until the wind no longer struck him and, assured that here was shelter of a sort, fought his way back to the top.

Again he plodded north until he reached the tethered mule. Untying the animal, he mounted and attempted to ride back to the flock against the wind. The wind was his only guide, his only landmark. To find his sheep again he must go squarely into the wind. The mule refused to face it, balking stubbornly.

Once more Dan dismounted. Once more he tied the mule. Now, on foot, he took his last desperate gamble. Squarely into the wind he walked; head bent, shoulders bowed, strong legs surging, he leaned against the storm and fought it. If the herd had changed direction in the least, if the wind had swung, he was lost and walking to certain death. Dan Shea did not think of that. He thought only of the sheep and the men as he fought the wind, his compass and his only guide.

Exhaustion came upon him, and he forced it back. His legs were leaden weights, ending in other weights that were his feet. These slipped on stones and tripped on sage. Twice he fell and forced himself up to go on into the wind-driven snow. Surely he had come far enough. Surely he had walked a great-enough distance to meet the herd. Panic swept over Dan Shea. Had he missed them? Were they to his right? To his left? Should he turn and circle, trying to find the herd? He fought the panic back. He must go on, straight into the wind.

Straight into the wind. Straight into the . . . He tripped again, falling forward. The thing that had tripped him scrambled and kicked. His arms gripped a woolly, snow-wet back. With a shout Dan Shea hauled himself up, his exhaustion and his panic lost in sheer gladness.

They turned the sheep a trifle. Working along the northern side of the drifting herd, whipping with sacks, rattling cans, aided and abetted by the dogs, they changed the course as Dan directed, Hilario and Nopomencenco and their companions. As they neared the canyon edge Dan led the way with Vicente. The leaders of the flock entered the narrow defile of the crevasse, and the herders plunged into the mass of sheep, breaking the pressure, thinning the herd from a marching mass into a thinner line. Vicente and Cercencio went down with the leaders, and endlessly the herd moved into the defile, driven by the storm, only partially controlled by the herders. Behind the herd came the camp burros, and Dan's mule joined them. Dan was the last of the men. Down into the crevasse they went, not knowing what was happening at the farther end, not knowing if the leaders had found a sheer drop and gone off, certain of but one thing: that here was shelter from the storm.

The sheep went on, the burros and the mule with them. Dan Shea and his herders followed them, endlessly it seemed, and the snow fell straight down, while above the canyon the wind howled its rage at being cheated. Then there was a disturbance, and a man broke through the sheep and, passing the camp animals, made his way to Dan Shea. Vicente it was, rimed with snow and grinning.

The little side canyon they followed, entered on a bench, Vicente informed. He and Cercencio had turned the leaders—now no longer driven by the wind—and held them on the bench. Vicente's grin was a beautiful thing to Dan Shea.

They followed the smiling little native. The last of the sheep and the burros and the mule cleared the mouth of the crevasse, and truly, as Vicente had said, there was a bench below the canyon rim. It stretched to north and south below the black-rimmed lip above. On it the sheep, huddled together, stood and looked at their saviors with black-slotted, foolish yellow eyes. Dan Shea sat down upon a snow-covered rock and looked up at a leaden sky through which the snow fell straight down.

By morning the storm was gone. The sky was a bright blue crease above the Rio Grande, and all the world was white. The crevasse that had offered them sanctuary was choked with snow, and the sheep, hungry, stirred restlessly.

With Dan's help the men broke through the drifts in the crevasse, driving the mules and burros back and forth until a trail was made. Then slowly, carefully, using all their knowledge and patience, they started the ewes up the trail that had been broken.

Before the bench was cleared two sheep had fallen from the brink of the ledge, crowded off by their sisters. Dan Shea looked back along its trampled length. The bench had saved him. He thought of that and was thankful. Then, turning, he followed the last of his men and animals toward the top.

For three, four, five weary days the herd crept over the drifted sage-dotted plain. Mountains towered above them on their left. Ahead was their destination: Colorado and the San Luis Valley. Three months behind them was El Puerto del Sol. This was the last stage, the finish of their journey.

On the sixth day after the storm Dan left his herd and rode north alone, traveling rapidly. That night he stayed with a native family, sleeping on the dirt floor of an adobe house. The next day brought him to the little clump of buildings, the store and the long warehouse and shed that was San Luis. Clambering down from his mule, Dan Shea tied her to the hitch rail in front of the store. Bearded, dirty and disheveled, he entered the building and, walking along its length, came finally to the little office in the rear. He stood in the doorway of the office, and behind his desk Sol Haberman looked up at his unkempt visitor.

"Remember me?" Dan Shea said to the swarthy, black-bearded man. "Do you remember me, Mr Haberman?"

Haberman shook his head. Behind Dan the store stretched away, the clerks busy with customers, dry goods on the shelves, groceries and staples filling the counters. Against that setting Dan Shea was an anomaly, a paradox, a heathen in a church.

"I'm Dan Shea. Last year in Denver you talked to me about bringing up a bunch of sheep from New Mexico to the valley. I've come and I've brought the sheep."

Haberman jumped up from behind the desk. "I remember," he said as he advanced. "You're Dan Shea. You had a freight outfit, and the panic wiped you out. I remember now."

The two shook hands. Haberman led Dan into the office and seated him beside the desk. He gave Dan a cigar. He jumped up again to put fresh wood on the fire in the stove and he asked questions. Dan relaxed in the chair and answered.

"But it's wintertime," Haberman said when the first questioning was finished. "How do you expect to sell sheep in the winter?"

Dan grinned. "You've hay," he answered. "I saw plenty of hay as I came in to town. I've got a band of ewes, Mr Haberman. I'll sell them cheap enough."

"How many an' how cheap?"

"About forty-eight hundred, and I'll let them go at six dollars."

Haberman threw up his hands. "Six dollars! Do you want to ruin me? I'll give you three."

Dan Shea grinned beneath his matted beard. Haberman wanted the sheep. Dan had been right. "I'll take five seventy-five," Dan said.

"But it's wintertime. I haven't got the hay. I can't do that."

Dan stirred in his chair as though to arise. "I've come so far with the sheep," he said carefully, "I can take them on. I can peddle them a little bunch at a time to the settlers north of here. If I have to I can take them clear to Denver. Five dollars and a half a head, Mr Haberman. Take it or leave it." Dan Shea got up.

"Sit down!" Haberman exclaimed. "Sit down, Mr Shea. Let's talk business. Five dollars and a half a head is too much. Think of the risk I take."

"Think of the risk I've taken," Dan Shea retorted. "Forty-eight hundred young ewes. Not a broken mouth in the bunch. They're thin but they're strong. And there's all that hay to feed them. What will you offer, Mr Haberman?"

"We'll go and see the sheep," Haberman said. "How far from town are they, Mr Shea?"

"They're this side of Costilla Plaza," Dan Shea answered. "We can see them tomorrow."

"You come to my house," Haberman invited. "You spend the night with me, Mr Shea. Mamma will feed you good and you'll sleep in a good bed. Tomorrow we'll see the sheep, an' maybe I'll give you three dollars and a half."

The following morning Dan Shea and Sol Haberman drove out of San Luis in Haberman's buggy, Dan's mule hitched to the hames of the off horse of the team and trotting along. There was no snow in the valley as yet, but clouds hung over the mountains above Costilla Peak and over San Antonio Mountain. Late that afternoon they reached the sheep and sat in the buggy while the ewes came slowly past. And that night at the sheep camp they renewed their bargaining. All next day as the two returned to San Luis the bargaining continued, and that evening in Haberman's office an agreement was concluded. Dan Shea sold his sheep to Sol Haberman at four dollars and seventy-five cents a head, Haberman to take a ten-per-cent cut of the flock and buy the cuts at three dollars and a half. Well content, the two men crossed from the store to Haberman's house where Mrs Haberman and a hot meal awaited them.

CHAPTER THIRTEEN:
OUT OF THE STORM

George Delaney was a pleasant man and cunning. When in 1865 he received his discharge from the Union army he looked about him and then decided that wealth and opportunity lay to the south. One of a myriad of carpetbaggers, he descended upon the unfortunate remnants of the Confederacy and for a time grew fat. But Texas, as a dwelling place, was hot for carpetbaggers. Hooded men rode at night with whips and weapons. Delaney saw the handwriting on the wall and migrated. Bendición was his stopping place.

The pickings in Bendición were lean, but Delaney readily made acquaintances and friends. A small case, a matter of a mining claim west of the river, fell into his hands, and he did much with it. Other cases followed. Then, searching among the archives in Santa Fe for a land title, he came upon the record of adjudication of El Puerto del Sol. Intrigued, Delaney read the old Spanish record through.

At first it offered no particular significance to him, then when he had returned to Bendición he fell to thinking. Delaney was acquainted with Ramon de la Luz. Idly, an idea stirring in his mind, he cultivated that acquaintanceship. From Ramon he had the story of the quarrel between the De la Luz family and the Alarids. Delaney pondered that tale. Gradually, because his mind was warped and twisted and shrewd, he evolved a plan. When the time was ripe he put that plan in motion.

The clan of De la Luz had pursued a course directly opposite to that Martin O'Connor followed. Where by strength, by ruthlessness, by purchase and by fear O'Connor had consolidated El Puerto del Sol, the De la Luzes, by procrastination, weakness and lack of foresight, squandered their heritage and split it into many small parts. Ramon de la Luz, the youngest, smartest and therefore the most discontented of all the clan, was the leader of his people. Heredity and ability made him so. When in the spring, just prior to Dan Shea's advent in Bendición, George Delaney, smooth and suave, spoke to Ramon concerning the possibility of regaining the northern portion of El Puerto del Sol, Ramon rose to the bait like a trout to a fly.

Having made an agreement with Ramon, having drawn up a cunning contract for Ramon's signature and locked it in his office safe, Delaney proceeded with his scheme. It was characteristic of the man that he would not take chances unless necessary. There were tools that he could use, and Delaney used them. It was natural, too, that when the tool had been used, or when it became dangerous to him, Delaney should discard or destroy it. While Dan Shea drove five thousand ewes north toward the Colorado market George Delaney sat in his office in Bendición or strolled about the plaza of the little town, apparently inactive, apparently harmless, but actually as dangerous as a coiled rattlesnake. Almost three months from the day of Dan's departure Delaney sat behind his desk, basking in the early winter sun. A knock upon his door aroused him and, rising, he strode across the office to answer the summons. When he opened the door and saw his visitor he stepped back.

"Come in, Tom," he welcomed.

A bearded man, heavy bodied, entered the office and closed the door. Delaney led the way to his desk.

"You sent word out you wanted to see me," Tom Warms announced, ridding himself of heavy coat and cap. "What's on your mind, Delaney?"

Delaney sat down, tipping back in his chair. Tom Warms also seated himself. "I've got several things on my mind," Delaney answered. "I sent word out three or four days ago for you to come in."

Warms frowned. "I didn't get it till yesterday," he said. "I was at the claim."

Neither man spoke for a moment, and Delaney teetered back and forth in his chair. "I've got a job for you," he said suddenly, his voice sharp.

"Yeah?" Warms said without enthusiasm.

"I want you to get rid of Dan Shea." Delaney let the chair come down on all four legs. "You've had a chance or two at him; this time I want you to get him."

Warms scowled. "Shea's a lucky bastard," he growled. "I had him dead to rights one time, an' Louder come chargin' up an' . . ."

"Never mind what Louder did," Delaney interrupted. "I know all about that. This time I want you to get Dan Shea."

Warms sat back in his chair. "What's in it?" he demanded bluntly. "Look here, Delaney, you don't go whippin' me into things without payin' me for it. What's in this for me?"

Delaney's voice became soft and smooth. "The little matter of dodging a murder charge," he answered, "and some money if you do the job."

Tom Warms's frown deepened. "Shea's unlucky to fool with," he growled. "He killed Lem up there at the San Felice stage stop an' he scared Tuttle so bad he left the country. I don't like to fool with Shea by myself."

"You'll have help," Delaney promised. "There's a boy here in town, Buster Flint, that has reason to hate Shea. He'll go with you."

Warms nodded. "I know Buster," he agreed. "He's all right. But look here, Delaney, you promised me when we got rid of Maples for you that you'd lay off. You was goin' to forget all about that business of me killin' Jefferson. You promised you'd give me that paper I signed admittin' I killed him. You ain't done it. You . . ." Tom Warms's voice was growing menacing with his anger.

Delaney slid his hand into the drawer of his desk and, bringing it out, rested his elbow on the desk top. His gun-filled hand lay carelessly on the papers that littered the desk.

"Cool down, Tom," he grated ominously. "I could kill you right here and go free. That confession isn't dated, remember. If I shot you in self-defense and showed that confession to Youtsey the whole country would give me a vote of thanks. You're going to do what I tell you, and I'm not going to give you back your confession. I'll keep it for insurance." Delaney laughed, an evil, mirthless chuckle. "And if something should happen to me," he concluded, "the officers would find that note of yours in my safe and they'd hang you, Tom. Hang you high and dry."

Tom Warms slumped back into his chair. His eyes, little and red rimmed and dark with anger, fixed themselves on Delaney's face. "You got me foul," Warms growled. "What is it you want me to do, Delaney? I tell you, messin' with Shea is bad luck, an' you're goin' to have to pay me for it."

"I'll pay you," Delaney promised. "Now listen, Tom. Carefully."

There in the warmth of his office, while the sunlight crawled across the floor, George Delaney drawled on. Tom Warms listened, now and again asking a question, now and again nodding his understanding.

"So that's what you'll do," Delaney finished. "I thought at first I'd send you out to stop him when he went north. Then I thought that this was a better plan. It's easier to stop one man alone than it is a bunch. You'll have Buster to take with you. Do you understand?"

Warms hoisted himself out of his chair. "I'll go talk to Buster," he growled. "After I talk to him I'll come back."

Delaney nodded. "Do that," he agreed. "But don't forget what I've got in my safe, Tom."

Warms went out and, smiling tightly, Delaney slipped his revolver back into the desk drawer.

He had hardly finished the movement before the door opened again and Ramon de la Luz, eyes angry, came storming into the office. He did not wait for a greeting but came straight to the desk, blurting words as he walked.

"O'Connor is going to Albuquerque. I have just

heard. There is something wrong. He will trick us . . ."

"Easy, Ramon," Delaney soothed. "Sit down and tell me about it."

Ramon de la Luz sat down. So much he conceded to Delaney's request. As for the rest, words poured from him. He had seen Martin O'Connor and Salvador Ocano in Bendición. Even now they were in the plaza, seated in O'Connor's buckboard. By inquiry Ramon had learned that the two were en route to Albuquerque. The information excited him. He poured out conjecture and suspicion to Delaney.

Delaney held up his hand for silence. "You've no need to worry, Ramon," he comforted. "No need at all. We'll go to Albuquerque ourselves. We'll leave right away. We'll be where we can watch him."

So pacified, Ramon calmed. Sardonically Delaney smiled at the man. If Ramon but knew it, Martin O'Connor was not the man to fear, nor were O'Connor's moves those that menaced.

"We'll take horses," Delaney said. "If O'Connor's traveling in his wagon we should beat him into Albuquerque by a day. Don't worry, Ramon. We'll take care of Martin O'Connor."

So it was that when at noon Martin O'Connor's canvas-covered wagon rolled out of Bendición and turned toward the north there were horsemen on the road, pushing along ahead of him. And so it was that when the equipage reached Albuquerque Ramon de la Luz and George Delaney were already registered at the hotel, awaiting his arrival.

O'Connor's trip to Albuquerque was caused by a sudden decision. Never one to lay aside responsibility or place it in another's hands, Don Martin had been distrait and moody since the day of Dan Shea's departure. Time hung heavily upon his hands, and inaction made the time seem longer. Marillita was no comfort for her father. She missed Dan and moped about the house, silent and mournful.

The letters that Dan wrote from Albuquerque cheered both the girl and her father, and for a few days after their arrival the two—father and daughter—were more nearly their former selves. Then during a visit to Bendición, O'Connor again encountered Ramon de la Luz on the plaza. The meeting was brief and hostile. Warm words led to other, hotter words, and only the intervention of friends kept the two men apart. O'Connor returned fuming to El Puerto del Sol, and the long wait began once more.

That waiting became intolerable. Action was O'Connor's life, and there was no action. Letters to Gotleib, even Gotleib's brief visit to the hacienda, did not bring surcease and so, suddenly, Martin O'Connor decided to go to Albuquerque, believing that his presence there would hasten events, certain that if he was on the scene he could accomplish what he wanted.

Marillita was to accompany her father on the trip, but the day prior to O'Connor's departure Esme Perrier appeared at El Puerto del Sol. It was Perrier's custom to spend the Christmas season with the O'Connors, and he was a welcome guest. Still all plans and preparations for the trip north were made, and O'Connor would not forgo it. He left Marillita to entertain their guest and, taking Salvador Ocano for company, started on his journey.

Martin O'Connor did not achieve his purpose in Albuquerque, and neither did Ramon de la Luz and

George Delaney. O'Connor, visiting with Bruno Gotleib, was assured that affairs were progressing as well as could be expected. Gotleib was still searching and having records searched for El Puerto del Sol's adjudication. So far he had not been successful. He promised faithfully that he would keep Don Martin informed, but he made it evident that O'Connor's presence was more hindrance than help, and Don Martin, realizing that he could do nothing, again sought release in action. He cut his stay in the northern town to one short day and began his return journey home.

As for Delaney and Ramon, they could learn nothing. They knew that O'Connor visited Gotleib, and that was all. There was no evidence of new action on Gotleib's part, and so, having assured Ramon that all was well and that O'Connor was not stealing a march upon them, Delaney could see no point in their staying further. As when the two parties left Bendición, so, too, the horsemen preceded the canvas-covered buckboard on the return journey.

Arturo de la Luz, that same Arturo of the shearers' camp at Rancho Norte, had come north with Delaney and Ramon. Arturo was Ramon's cousin, his *primo*, and since the encounter between Martin O'Connor and himself in Bendición's plaza, Ramon had kept Arturo with him as a sort of bodyguard.

The day was overcast and cloudy as the three men rode out from Albuquerque. A cold wind working around from the west settled in the north and blew steadily. Behind the riders the Sandias were hidden by clouds that hung low over their peaks, and by noon there was a steady, cutting drizzle coming with the wind. Before three o'clock the storm was in full sway, and, wet through and miserable, the travelers sought shelter.

The country was uninhabited. There were simply broad reaches of mesa stretching away on either hand, dotted with desert growth. The last stage stop was six miles behind them, the next a good ten miles ahead. Arturo, swinging close to Ramon, spoke of an old goat camp not half a mile off the road. If the goats and their herders were at the camp there would be food and warmth. If the camp was uninhabited it would still afford a place of refuge. Ramon and Delaney needed no urging. They turned their horses from the road and, following Arturo's lead, cut across the beating rain and wind toward the east.

The goat camp was a small rock house with a rock corral and a shed behind it. When the three arrived they found the house untenanted. There was no sign of recent occupancy. The door swung open readily under Ramon's hand, and the three stepped in upon the earthen floor, out of the wind.

In the gloom of the small room, out of the storm, the three men paused and held a consultation. There was a fireplace at the end of the room, dry wood left by the goatherds piled beside it. While Ramon worked with knife and flint and steel to kindle a fire Arturo went out into the storm to put the horses in the shed. He returned to find a tiny blaze snapping on the hearth and Delaney and Ramon laying aside their coats and making themselves as comfortable as possible. Arturo, too, removed his worn coat and hung it from a peg driven between the rocks of the wall. The coat dripped water on the hard-packed earthen floor. Arturo advanced to the fire. Delaney and Ramon were already before the fireplace, and as the fire grew the men turned, now toasting a steaming back, now extending their hands to the warming blaze. Water, falling down the chimney, hissed as it struck the flames. Occasionally a puff of wind, blowing down, spread cedar smoke into the room. Outside the rain, whipped by the wind, beat against the rock walls, and in one corner the sagging roof leaked and water came down in a tiny trickle to run across the floor toward the door.

Delaney grinned cheerfully at Ramon. "It's a good thing Arturo knew about this place," he said. "I was about frozen."

Ramon nodded. "We should have stayed in Albuquerque," he answered moodily.

Delaney shook his head. "No," he affirmed, "we should have stopped at the stage station. Well, we can get warm here, and when the rain lets up we'll go on. I want to get back to Bendición."

"I think . . ." Ramon began and stopped short. There were sounds other than those of wind and rain outside the rock house. Chains jangled. There was a rattle of wheels. Voices, indistinct and blurred by the walls, the wind and the rain, came to the men in the room.

"Somebody else knew about this place," Delaney said. "They've come to get out of the storm. I wonder who . . ."

Once more the door was thrust open, swinging back into the room. A man, big bodied, covered by a coat, his dripping hat pulled low, stood in the opening, his head turned so that he spoke across his shoulder to a companion outside.

"*Ándale*, Salvador," he ordered. Then Martin

O'Connor turned his head and stepped across the threshold.

In the dusk of the room O'Connor did not recognize the men beside the fire. He advanced toward the blaze, unbuttoning his coat as he moved, removing his hat and shaking the water from it. He had nearly reached the fireplace before his eyes, becoming accustomed to the dim light, focused on George Delaney. Then he stopped short and stared in disbelief.

Delaney spoke cheerfully. "Bad storm," he said. "We pulled out of it. How are you, Don Martin?"

For an instant O'Connor made no answer. He was of a mind to turn, go out into the storm again and, calling Salvador, continue his journey. But that thought was instantly discarded. Martin O'Connor had never in his lifetime retreated. To leave now would be a signal of retreat. He came on to the fire, letting his coat swing open.

"Take off your coat and dry out," Delaney counseled.

O'Connor stopped close by the blaze. He looked from Delaney to Ramon de la Luz and to Arturo who squatted on a corner of the hearth.

"Headed for Albuquerque?" Delaney asked casually.

"You know where I'm going," Martin O'Connor ground out.

Delaney shifted position. "I've been wanting to see you," he announced. "I wanted to talk to you about this suit."

"George . . ." Ramon began. "I believe . . ."

"Wait a minute, Ramon," Delaney ordered. "I'm talking to Don Martin. Mr O'Connor, there's no reason why we can't get together on this thing.

We've got you beat if it comes to trial. Why not save yourself expense and settle out of court?"

Salvador Ocano came in, closing the door behind him, paused and, pulling off his hat, shook off the water. The drops spattered sharply on the floor as he swung the felt. He took a step and then stopped, seeing and recognizing the men beside the fireplace.

"How about it, Mr O'Connor?" Delaney pursued the thought. "We're all right here and . . ."

"If I had known I was walking into a nest of rats I'd have gone on!" Martin O'Connor glared at the lawyer. "Damn you, Delaney! You're behind all this. You know that no damned De la Luz ever owned a foot of El Puerto del Sol!"

Delaney spread his hands. "Prove it!" he taunted. "You can't prove it, O'Connor. I'm trying to give you an out, man. You can settle . . ."

"I can settle you!" O'Connor roared. "You an' Ramon an' all of you. Let me get my hands on you . . ." He advanced a threatening step, his big hands reaching out. Delaney moved away. Ramon, shifting forward, dark face scowling, was before Martin O'Connor.

"*Cabrón,*" he snarled. "*Ladrón!*"

"Thief, is it?" O'Connor roared. "By God, I'll . . ." He moved swiftly toward Ramon, no question left of his intentions as his hands reached out. Ramon recoiled a step. There in the four rock walls a shot roared. Martin O'Connor staggered and fell back, his hand groping behind him for support. In front of the fireplace Ramon stood, his gun smoking. By the door Salvador Ocano shouted hoarsely and moved forward, two long steps.

From the hearth corner Arturo sprang up, his

knife glinting evilly. Salvador gave a long, bubbling scream that ended short, chopped off in mid-sound, seemed to rise on his toes as Arturo pressed against him and then collapsed into a huddle on the dirt floor. Martin O'Connor had fallen on his side. Now he moved a trifle, his heavy shoulders touching the dirt.

"That does it!" Delaney snarled. "You've killed him, Ramon!"

Ramon de la Luz stared down at the gun still in his hand, still with a thread of smoke trickling from the muzzle. Delaney, moving swiftly, reached O'Connor and, kneeling beside him, looked at the bearded face. Martin O'Connor's eyes were open, wide with shock and surprise.

"I'm hit," he muttered. "My leg won't work. Help me up."

Delaney got up and faced Ramon. "There was no need of this!" he snapped. "There were enough of us to stop him without shooting. You've torn it now. If we go into court . . ." He stopped. Still staring at Ramon, Delaney's face changed expression, the look that was on it, half fright, half anger, draining slowly away. Delaney turned a trifle and stared down at O'Connor, and a gleam of shrewd cunning came into his eyes.

"Maybe this is the best way after all," he exclaimed suddenly, as though he spoke to himself. "Shea's gone. There's just the girl. Maybe . . ." He broke off.

"Help me up," O'Connor ordered again, a new strength coming into his voice. "Can't you see I'm hurt? Help me up, I say!"

"I believe you were right, Ramon," Delaney said calmly. "This is the best way after all." His right hand reached into the pocket of his coat and reappeared holding a small derringer.

At sight of the gun Ramon de la Luz's eyes widened. "George!" he began. "What are you . . . ?"

"I'll finish what you started," Delaney snapped, sudden ferocity on his face. "You . . ." The derringer leveled. Martin O'Connor's eyes were wide with incredulity. Once again the walls of the rock house reverberated with the explosion of powder. One . . . two . . . the shots came deliberately, crashing and echoing in the little room. Delaney lowered the derringer and faced Ramon de la Luz.

"That settles that!" he snarled. "It's finished!"

CHAPTER FOURTEEN:
THE ROAD HOME

For almost a week after his first contact with Sol Haberman, Dan Shea stayed in the vicinity of San Luis. First the sheep had to be moved closer to the little town, and then came the delivery. Haberman was in no hurry and, sensing Dan's impatience, he took advantage of it. The merchant, having bought a bargain, sought to make the bargain better, and he quibbled and argued over the cutting of the herd and the terms of the agreement.

Haberman, strive as he would, could not stretch out the delivery indefinitely, and finally it was accomplished. The merchant paid for the ewes with a draft on a Trinidad bank. He did not have in cash the amount necessary to complete the transaction. Dan Shea wanted cash. He could not take the draft to Albuquerque and cash it there, for then the money would of necessity go into O'Connor's account, and there was still an attachment on the don's bank account. The best place to exchange the draft for money was in Trinidad. Whisky Pass, the road across the mountains from San Luis to Trinidad, was blocked with snow. It was necessary that Dan go another route.

Placing Hilario in charge of the herders, and with

fresh supplies purchased, Dan started them back along the trail. They were to go down through the valley, past Costilla, on to Arroyo Hondo and, crossing the river on the toll bridge, continue south, following the road in to Santa Fe, to Albuquerque and thence south to Bendición. In order to expedite the return Dan bought mounts for the herders. He himself, with Vicente to accompany him, struck south. At Costilla, above the plaza, they found the river low enough to ford. Crossing the river, they traveled southeast, bucking the snow and making a laborious progress across the mountains to the thriving mining center of Elizabethtown. From that place they had a good wagon road that led directly to Trinidad.

In Trinidad Dan encountered difficulty in cashing the draft. Dan Shea was not known to Haberman's bankers, and they demanded identification. Fortunately there were men in town who had known Shea in the days when he had operated a freighting outfit, and when these had identified him the draft was paid. Thus, with a fortune about his middle in a money belt, and with Vicente trotting along beside him on a mule, Dan Shea began the long journey home.

From Trinidad he climbed up, taking Wooton's toll road across Raton Pass, paying toll at the gate close beside the old pioneer's ranch house, dropping on down to the stage station at Willow Springs, following along the stage road through Springer, Wagon Mound, Las Vegas and on toward the south. He was cautious as he rode for he knew that travelers were not safe in the country and that he was a tempting bait for any robber. Restraining his impatience, he stopped when night came, making his journey only by daylight, taking no risks. Vicente was always beside him, bright-eyed, alert, his Springfield across his thighs as he rode. Vicente had grown. He was squat and broad shouldered and stout, and a dark fuzz was beginning to cover his face. Dan Shea was Vicente's god. At a word from Dan Vicente would have walked into hell itself and gone to grips with the devil.

There was snow in the mountains below Las Vegas. In places the road was blocked by drifts through which the two travelers fought their way. The days were short, and perforce the journey of the day was also short. Dan fumed with impatience. Marillita was at the end of the long road, pulling on the strings. Dan Shea could feel the tug of those strings. Restraint became more and more difficult. They reached Santa Fe, tarried there a night and then went on. Bernalillo was reached late in the day with the sun going down and the long winter darkness spreading all about. Albuquerque was but twelve miles from Bernalillo, two and a half hours' journey beyond them. Dan Shea cast caution to the winds. They would go on to Albuquerque. In Albuquerque was Bruno Gotleib and word from El Puerto del Sol. In Albuquerque there would be a letter from Marillita.

Vicente and Dan Shea ate a hasty supper in the stage tavern in Bernalillo. While they ate their meal the mules were fed. Intent upon continuing his journey, hurried, fretted by his own impatience, Dan Shea lost some of his alertness. He had told the tavern keeper, when that worthy made inquiry, that he would not stay the night but would push on; and in the dining room, engrossed in his meal, he did not see the bearded man that came to the tavern keeper and casually made inquiry concerning the white man and the Indian in the dining room. Nor did he see the bearded man turn away, his inquiry answered, and walk out into the night that surrounded the tavern.

His meal finished, with Vicente beside him like a shadow, Dan Shea sought the barn. The mules had been fed, the hostler said there in the warmth of the stable. It was a cold night and the weather was unsettled. There was a storm in prospect. Dan Shea, tightening the cinch about his mule, paid scant heed to the hostler's warning. As he mounted, Vicente, too, found his saddle, and side by side the two left the lights and movement of Bernalillo. Before them stretched El Camino Real, the King's Highway. Twelve miles more and they would be in Albuquerque, their journey almost done!

Vicente's mule was weary, more tired than the mule that Dan bestrode. Vicente's mule, with the stubbornness of the breed, kept dropping back. Dan Shea, perforce, halted from time to time and waited for his companion to catch up. Sometimes in his impatience Dan did not notice that Vicente lagged and went on a distance before he stopped. The night was dark, with a ringed moon that gave but small light. Half an hour out of Bernalillo snow began to fall, great, wet flakes that melted when they struck Dan's face and formed a thin white collar on his coat.

Vicente had dropped back and Dan was perhaps fifty yards in advance when the call came. From beside the road, in the shadow of the great, gaunt cottonwoods that towered skyward, a voice lifted.

"Hey there! Hey, stranger!"

Dan Shea stopped his mule. He was alert, the

thoughts that had engrossed him lost in the immediate awakening. "What's wanted?" he called.

"I got some trouble here," the voice answered plaintively. "Wagon's broke down. Can you give me a hand?"

"I'm in a hurry," Dan answered. "Can't stop." As he spoke he unbuttoned his outer coat. Vicente had stopped at the hail, just as Dan had done. He was back there on the road, waiting. Dan's coat swung open and his hand reached in to the butt of the Colt holstered beneath his arm. He was alarmed.

"Will you take word into town for me then?" Again the voice came from the shadow of the cottonwoods. "I got to have some help. Broke the reach on my wagon an' . . ." A lone man was coming out of the shadows toward Dan. Instinctively Dan relaxed. One man complaining about a broken wagon reach could not be very dangerous.

"I'll take in word," Dan agreed. "Who do you want me to tell?"

"You can tell the hostler at the OK wagon yard," the advancing man answered. "You can . . ."

He broke his speech and moved swiftly, almost beside Dan Shea. His hand shot up, gripping Dan's coat and jerking, hauling Dan down from the mule. Behind Dan Shea, in the darkness, Vicente stirred to action. Vicente's Springfield, carried across his thighs, was immediately available. The Springfield boomed, flame ringing its muzzle, blindingly. There was a frightened squawl from the ditch beside the road, the ditch that the cottonwoods shadowed, and momentarily the man that struggled with Dan Shea stopped his tugging.

That moment gave Dan his chance. His hand came out from beneath his coat, the Colt cocked and gripped firmly. He thrust the Colt down, its muzzle touching cloth, and pulled the trigger. The man who held him grunted and released his hold, staggering back. Dan came off the mule, tumbling from the little beast. He sensed rather than heard Vicente go by, running on foot. Then he was at grips with the man he had shot, tumbling over him, the pistol upraised in his hand as he sought for a place to strike.

The gun chopped down, thudding on cloth and flesh, chopped down again. Beyond Dan there was a flurry of sound, a squeak as frightened as the sound of a mouse when the cat pounces, then the dull roar of a shot. Dan swung the Colt again, struck and heard the gun crunch against bone. Beneath him his adversary slumped, relaxed and lay quiet. There were footsteps close by and Dan, rising so that he was on his knees, pointed the gun in the direction of the sound, finger tense upon the trigger.

"Soy Vicente," came a voice.

Dan relaxed his finger on the trigger and then, thumb on hammer, uncocked the gun.

"El otro está muerto," Vicente announced with satisfaction.

Dan Shea got to his feet. With trembling fingers he sought and found a block of sulphur matches, pulled them out and, breaking off one match, struck it against the block. The match flamed an evil yellow. Bending, the match in his hand, Dan examined the man who had attacked him. A bearded, snarling face was upturned. Dan recognized that face. It was the man of the stage station of San Felice who had killed Maples, the man Dan had seen talking to George Delaney in Bendición's plaza.

The match guttered out. Vicente tugged at Dan's

sleeve. Together they walked to the ditch, and there
Dan Shea lit another match. This time he knew not
only the identity but the name of the man that Vicente had killed. It was Buster, the erstwhile rider
of Jesse Louder's YH. Vicente had used a knife, and
Buster was not a pretty sight. Retiring a short distance from the bodies, Shea and his companion
stood together. The mules were waiting patiently.
Involuntarily Dan Shea shivered. He was chilled
with a coldness other than that of the winter night.
This was no ordinary robbery, no common holdup.
These men had been sent; George Delaney had
sent them. Dan was sure of it, sure but could not
prove his facts.

"Señor . . ." Vicente wanted to know the next
move. He wanted Dan to make a decision. Dan
thought rapidly. They were almost halfway between Bernalillo and Albuquerque. Should they go
back? Dan shook his head. No use of going back.
He knew no one in Bernalillo. In Albuquerque
there was Bruno Gotleib.

"We'll go on," Dan announced. "Leave them
here, Vicente. We'll go on to Albuquerque."

They mounted the mules. Riding on toward the
south, the mules made a circle around the bodies
that lay beside the road. Vicente stared down at the
black blotch on the snow, the black blotch that was
Buster. Pride welled up in Vicente. He had proved
his worth. Dan Shea added to the pride.

"You're a good boy, Vicente," he said after riding
a long distance in silence.

Vicente straightened visibly, sat taller in his
saddle.

It was eleven o'clock when Albuquerque was
reached. Dan led the way directly to Bruno Gotleib's

house. That was the first place to report. When Gotleib was up and dressed they would go to the sheriff's office together, and Dan could tell his story then but not before. It would be a good thing to have Bruno Gotleib with him. Gotleib could vouch for Dan Shea to the officers.

The house stood in darkness. Dan left Vicente with the weary mules and, climbing the steps, battered on the door. Three times he knocked before a light appeared within the house. From behind the door a woman's voice came, muffled and frightened. "Who is it?"

"Dan Shea."

There was a brief pause, then the lock rattled. The door swung open and Mrs Gotleib, muffled in a long dressing robe, a lamp in her hand, stood facing Dan.

"Where's Mr Gotleib?" Dan asked hastily. "I've got to see him."

Mrs Gotleib shook her head. Her eyes were wide, filled with some emotion that Dan could not read. "Bruno isn't here," she said. "He's gone to El Puerto del Sol."

"To El Puerto del Sol?"

Slowly the woman nodded her head. "You haven't heard," she said, her voice filled with compassion. "You've been gone."

"Haven't heard what?" Dan demanded. "Tell me."

"Martin O'Connor was killed," Mrs Gotleib said. "Bruno's gone to El Puerto to do what he can. You'd better come in, Mr Shea."

Dan Shea put his hand against the doorjamb for support. "Killed?" he said, unbelievingly. "Why I . . ."

Mrs Gotleib stepped back. "Come in," she said gently. "Is there anyone with you?"

"Yes. There's Vicente. I . . ."

"Call him in. I'll tell you what I know, Mr Shea."

Dan called Vicente, ordering him to tie the mules and come. When Vicente had obeyed the two men followed Mrs Gotleib into the house. In the living room she placed the lamp on the table and, drawing her wrapper about her, sank into a chair. Dan Shea faced her, and Vicente remained beside the door, his face an expressionless mask.

"Mr O'Connor had been to see Bruno," Mrs Gotlieb began. "He was going home. He was caught in a storm evidently and took shelter in a goat camp. The herders found his body there. He'd been robbed. They brought him in to Albuquerque and Bruno was called. He's taken the body back to El Puerto del Sol. He left two days ago."

"Was anybody with Don Martin?" Dan asked, his voice strained.

"Salvador Ocano. He was killed too."

"Do they know . . . ? Is anyone suspected?"

Mrs Gotleib shook her gray head. "No one," she answered. "The sheriff thinks that Mr O'Connor was killed and robbed. He hasn't any idea who did it. Let me make you some coffee, Mr Shea. You're tired and this has been a shock to you. I'll . . ." She got up.

Dan held up a restraining hand. "I've got to get on to El Puerto del Sol," he said hoarsely. "I've got to go. Where can I get horses, Mrs Gotleib? I've got to go on now, tonight!"

Mrs Gotleib nodded understandingly. "I'll dress," she said. "Then I'll take you over to Mitchell

Kemp's. He's Bruno's clerk. He can help you get horses."

"Tell me where he lives," Dan ordered. "There's no need of your going out. I can . . ."

"No." Mrs Gotleib shook her head. "It won't take but a minute for me to dress. I'll go with you."

Morning light, gradually unfolding details of road and country, found Dan Shea and Vicente on the road below Albuquerque. They were riding horses rented from the stage line. At San Felice they would leave the mounts they bestrode and, taking fresh horses, go on. Both men were weary, tired through to the bone, but there was no stopping. A grim relentlessness kept Dan Shea upright in his saddle, and that force, derived from Dan, also kept Vicente going. Vicente dozed as he rode, his hands wrapped about his saddle horn, his head slumped to his chest. But Dan could neither relax nor rest at all.

At San Felice the change of horses was accomplished and the men rode on. It was impossible for them to reach Bendición before night came. Still, as evening grew they pushed steadily into the dusk. It was then that Vicente, riding close, spoke to his companion.

"Señor . . ."

"What is it, Vicente?"

"Do you think that Don Martin was killed by those men we met?"

Dan Shea shook his head. "I don't know," he answered. "I do think that those men and the men who killed Don Martin worked for the same man."

"Do you think we will meet that man?"

"I know we'll meet him," Dan Shea answered

with a grim sureness of tone. "I *know* that, Vicente."

Vicente reined his horse away and rode on. He was content.

The hours went past with the miles. Night came and the horses followed the road in the moonlight. Then in the moonlight the black spot that was Bendición showed and gradually grew nearer, resolving into houses, into the skeletons of trees, into sparks of light. Wearily Dan Shea and Vicente turned their horses into the plaza. There were lights about the plaza, glowing from the buildings, from the Golden Horn, from Fitzpatrick's saloon, from the hotel. In front of Fitzpatrick's the horses stopped, and stiffly the riders dismounted. With Vicente following him Dan pushed open the door and stepped into the barroom. At the bar a customer, taking one last drink, looked up quickly at the sound of arrival. Behind the bar Fitzpatrick said: "I'll be damned. It's Dan!"

Dan Shea leaned wearily against the doorjamb. "It's me, Fitz," he agreed. "I've had the word. I've got to get out to El Puerto del Sol."

Fitzpatrick came around the end of the bar. "You're tuckered out," he announced. "Wouldn't tomorrow mornin' do? Can't you wait?"

Dan shook his head. "Tonight," he said hoarsely. "I've got to . . ." Fitzpatrick caught Dan as he slumped down and, supporting him, helped his friend to a chair.

"You can't go tonight," he objected. "You're pooped out, Dan."

"I've got to go tonight."

Fitzpatrick straightened. Vicente had slumped wearily into a chair and was already asleep, his head resting on his arms where they sprawled out on a table. "Then I'll take you out," Fitzpatrick announced. "I'll get a team from the livery barn an' drive you."

"It's mighty good of you, Fitz," Dan Shea said, and utter exhaustion showed in his voice. "I . . . I think I'll sleep a little while you get the team." Every word had been an effort. Now, with the sentence spoken, Dan Shea, too, leaned forward on the table and, like Vicente, rested his head on his extended arms.

Fitzpatrick looked at his solitary customer. "Jack," he directed, "you stay here an' look after things awhile, will you? I'm closed up for the night. I'll be right back."

The customer nodded and Fitzpatrick, taking his coat from a hook on the back wall, pulled it on and hurried out into the night.

CHAPTER FIFTEEN:
YELLOW PARCHMENT

Fitzpatrick brought a buggy from the livery barn. There was not room in the buggy for three people, and so when he wakened Dan and helped the sleep-numbed man out to the waiting rig, Fitzpatrick did not disturb Vicente. With the help of the man who had stayed at the saloon Fitzpatrick carried Vicente to a cot in the back room and placed him there, Vicente sleeping deeply throughout the whole proceeding.

"You tell my bartender to look out for him, Jack," Fitzpatrick admonished his companion. "He'll be all right there for now, but he'd drink all the liquor in the place if somebody wasn't with him when he woke up. An' tell the bartender I'll be back when I get here an' he's to look after things."

Jack said: "Sure thing, Fitz."

"An' take these horses down to the livery," Fitzpatrick ordered. "I forgot 'em. Here . . . wait till I get the stuff off the saddles."

He was standing in the door of his saloon as he spoke and now he stepped out to the horses, lifted Dan's saddlebags from behind one saddle and, untying saddle strings, took Vicente's bundle from behind the cantle of the other saddle. "I'll lock up," he said. "An' I'm sure obliged to you, Jack."

"That's all right, Fitz," Jack said.

A key clicked in the lock of the door, and Fitzpatrick climbed into the waiting buggy where Dan Shea, utterly worn, slept soundly. Jack waited until the buggy rolled away and then, taking the bridle reins, started down the side of the plaza, leading the horses.

Fitzpatrick drove steadily. He had moonlight until the bridge was crossed. After the moon set he continued, the horses following the well-marked road; Fitzpatrick relaxed under the darkness of the buggy's top.

Gray dawn was in the east when Fitzpatrick's buggy wheeled into the settlement of El Puerto del Sol. He drove up the hill, stopped the buggy in front of the big house and, reaching for Dan's shoulder, shook it.

"Wake up, Dan!" Fitzpatrick ordered. "Wake up. We're here."

Dan opened his eyes and stared blankly at his friend. Then as realization dawned, overpowering sleep, he straightened, shifted on the seat and stepped down from the buggy.

El Puerto del Sol was not yet awake. Dan Shea, with Fitzpatrick beside him, beat upon a door until it was opened and the sleepy face of the *mayordomo* showed. That face brightened as the arrivals were recognized, and the *mayordomo* brought the two men into the living room of the big house and hastened away to arouse the occupants of the hacienda. Dan sank down in a chair. Fitzpatrick walked over and stood looking out a window. Muffled voices sounded, then Bruno Gotlieb, his nightshirt tucked into his trousers, and slippers on his sockless feet, entered the room.

"You heard?" he asked, looking at Dan.

"In Albuquerque," Dan answered. "I came right on. How is Marillita?"

"She's taking it badly," Gotleib answered. "She . . ." He stopped. Swift steps sounded. Marillita, a dressing gown thrown over her night robe, appeared at the door, paused a moment and then with a little cry ran across the long room to Dan. Gotleib turned away. Fitzpatrick, after one hasty glance, faced the window again. There was no sound in the room other than the soft weeping of the girl.

Gradually her sobbing quieted. Lifting his face from Marillita's hair, Dan saw Gotleib and Fitzpatrick watching him, compassion in their expressions. There were two others in the room: Perrier, the Englishman, and a short, small-bodied man dressed in the robes of a priest. The priest advanced, his face sad and yet somehow lifting the sorrow that weighted Dan. The priest reached out his hand and gently touched Marillita.

"He has come a long way," the priest said softly. "He needs rest and food, Marillita."

It was exactly the right thing to have said. The girl straightened, recalled from her grief. "Of course," she said. "Oh, Dan . . ."

A moment more she remained in Dan's arms, as though loath to leave their consolation. Then, freeing herself, she hastened across the room and out the door. The priest stood looking at Dan Shea. "I am Father John, my son," he announced, holding out his hand.

Dan took the proffered hand in his own. He

shook hands with Bruno Gotleib and received and
returned a firm handgrip with Perrier. Marillita
came back into the room to cross and stand beside
Dan. He slipped his arm around her, and there was
an awkward silence. While the girl was present
Dan could not ask the questions that filled him.
Father John sensed that. Once more he came forward and touched Marillita.

"Come," he ordered, "the men must talk." Obe-
diently Marillita followed him, looking back at Dan
Shea from the door. When priest and girl were
gone Dan sat down.

"You'll want to know what happened," Gotleib
announced, his tone clipped and short. "I'll tell
you." He, too, seated himself. Perrier found a chair.
Fitzpatrick remained standing, staring moodily out
the window.

"I brought Don Martin back yesterday," Gotleib
began. "I came in yesterday afternoon." With that
beginning he continued, telling Dan of the finding
of two bodies by goatherders who came to shelter
following a storm; of how those herders had sent
for officers; of the identification of the bodies; of
how he had been informed, and of what had been
done. Halfway through, an interruption checked
the recital. Fitzpatrick turned from the window and
made a brief announcement. "Here's Louder."

Gotleib paused while Perrier went to the door
and ushered lanky Jesse Louder into the room.
Louder shook hands with Dan, with Perrier and
with Gotleib and made brief announcement. "I got
the word last night. Came over as quick as I could."
He sat down, and Gotleib, going back, retraced
what he had already told and then continued to the
completion of his tale.

"No one knows who did it," Gotleib concluded. "There were no tracks. The rain had washed them out. Whoever killed Don Martin left no clues. But . . ." The lawyer paused a moment.

"Go on, man!" Dan Shea ordered.

"Ramon de la Luz and George Delaney were in Bendición just before the bodies were found," Gotleib announced. Then significantly: "They'd been in Albuquerque but they weren't there when the word was brought in."

Dan Shea grunted, like a man hit low, below the belt. His eyes traveled around the little circle and paused upon Gotleib's face.

"Of course that proves nothing," Gotleib interposed hastily.

"I want you to know," Louder said in the silence that followed Gotleib's statement, "that I'm with you in whatever you do, Shea."

Dan turned to look at the cowman. Louder was watching him intently, as were all the others. It was borne to Dan Shea then that these men, all of them, were with him. Louder had simply voiced the thoughts of all. They would follow him, Louder, Fitzpatrick, Perrier, even Gotleib. The leadership was his.

"I . . ." Dan Shea began. Then: "We'll take things one at a time." He paused a moment as though he would speak further, then abruptly he got up and left the room.

Marillita was in the little chapel. Martin O'Connor lay in state before the altar and, as was fitting, Salvador Ocano lay beside him. El Puerto del Sol had furnished two diamond-shaped wooden coffins for these, her master and her son. Tall candles burned about the biers, and Marillita knelt before the altar.

Dan Shea joined her. They were both there, kneeling side by side, when Father John, robed in his vestments, roused them gently and led them to the family pew. The little church filled with silent men and women, and the strong deep voice of the priest as he began to intone the Latin of the Mass echoed in the quiet.

From the tiny chapel, through the cold December morning, the men of El Puerto del Sol carried Martin O'Connor to his final resting place. Salvador Ocano followed his *patrón,* in death as in life, and in the burial ground Martin O'Connor was lowered beside his wife. Again the priest spoke, completing the ritual, asking a final blessing on these servants of the Church, and presently the graveyard was emptied as the procession filed away, Marillita leaning heavily upon Dan Shea's arm.

Back at the house once more Perrier and Fitzpatrick, Louder and Gotleib, gathered in the living room. Father John joined them there.

"Dan?" Fitzpatrick said, questioning the priest.

"He's with Marillita," Father John replied.

Fitzpatrick nodded and sat down. The others also found seats. A fire snapping in the fireplace broke the heavy silence of the wait. Father John looked at the men. Their faces were hard, stern with the thoughts of their owners. The priest sighed. He could guess those thoughts.

"I wish Dan would come," Fitzpatrick said restlessly when the wait had grown intolerable.

"He'll come soon enough," Perrier answered, his words clipped. "And he'll tell us."

As though that were his cue Dan Shea came through the door and stopped. "Marillita's resting," he announced. "I persuaded her to lie down." Every eye in the room was fixed on Dan's face.

"Well, Shea?" Louder rasped.

Dan came on into the room and sank heavily into a chair beside the fireplace. Mechanically he reached down and, lifting a log from the pile beside the hearth, placed it on the flames.

"I sold the sheep," he announced suddenly. "I'll tell you."

The others leaned forward, all save the priest who stood watching them.

"I've brought the money home," Dan continued. "Not that it will do any good now." His voice was bitter. "I sold the sheep to Haberman in the San Luis Valley."

There was no inflection in his voice as he continued. Dispassionately, as though he spoke of some immaterial thing, Dan Shea recounted the story of his northward journey. When he told of the Apache raid and of the vengeance he had exacted his voice rose a trifle, dropping back into its monotony when that portion of the tale was finished. The long trip north passed before Dan's listeners in his terse, quiet account. The bargaining with Haberman, the final delivery of the sheep, the trip to Trinidad: all these were passed over swiftly, simply.

"So I got the money," Dan Shea completed. "I traveled days because I wanted to get it here safe. When we got to Bernalillo I got impatient. We came on that night. Below Bernalillo we were jumped by two men. One of them was the man who killed Maples. Remember, Fitz? I said I'd seen him with Delaney in the plaza."

Fitzpatrick nodded.

"The other"—Dan turned to Louder—"used to

work for you. His name was Buster Something-or-other."

"Buster Flint," Louder amended. "Go on, Shea."

"They tried to waylay us," Dan recounted. "Vicente was behind. His mule was tired and he'd dropped back. He came up, and that gave me a chance and I took the fellow that had jumped me. Vicente got to this Buster Flint and killed him. We came on to Albuquerque. I was going to report the whole thing to the sheriff, but when I got to your house, Gotleib, I heard about Don Martin so I came on here."

His recital finished, Dan looked at his friends. A little silence hung over the group. "That's all of it, then," Fitzpatrick broke the quiet. "What do you think, Dan?"

"What you all think," Dan answered swiftly. "But I haven't got a dime's worth of proof."

"Hell," Louder drawled, "we don't need proof."

Fitzpatrick placed the tips of his long fingers together. "The man that killed Maples," he said slowly. "He tried for you an' you got him. Dan, I've always wondered why Maples was killed. If that damned Lucero up at the stage station hadn't sloped with Maples' grip mebbe we'd of found out. He . . ."

Suddenly Dan Shea straightened. "What did you say?" he demanded.

"I was talkin' about Maples," Fitzpatrick reminded patiently. "I said if that hostler, Lucero, hadn't run off with Maples' grip mebbe we'd of known what that was all about."

In Dan's mind events fell into place, seemingly clicked into a pattern. Maples! Lucero! He could almost picture the campfire with Landcaster, the scout, lounging beside it; could almost hear the old scout's drawling voice: "Lucero was a half-breed an' clear bad. He'd worked with white men just long enough to get smart. I knew there'd be trouble when he come back to the reservation last spring."

"I wish Vicente was here," Dan said. "He's got some stuff in his bundle that I wish I had."

"I brought it out last night," Fitzpatrick stated, rising. "It's around someplace. Mebbe in the buggy."

Dan's eyes brightened. "Get it," he ordered and then, looking at Father John: "Can you read Spanish, Padre?"

"Yes," the priest answered, puzzled. "I can read it."

"Get that bundle, Fitz!" Dan Shea commanded.

Fitzpatrick went out. While he was gone the men eyed Dan Shea with puzzled eyes. They sensed his excitement, sensed the pent-up tension in the man. "What's this all about, Shea?" Louder asked finally. "What's got you stirred up?"

"I don't know for sure," Dan responded. "I think . . . Here's Fitz!"

Fitzpatrick came back carrying Vicente's blanket-wrapped bundle. He dumped it down on a table top without regard for the polished surface. "There you are, Dan," Fitzpatrick said.

Dan's fingers fumbled as he untied knots in a buckskin string. He spread the bundle open, exposing Vicente's few personal belongings, exposing a battered derby hat, a wrinkled coat with a loud pattern, bringing to light a long roll of leather. Still with fumbling fingers he opened the roll and brought out parchments which he held out toward Father John.

"Can you read this?" Dan demanded.

The priest took the parchments, yellow and crackling. He looked at the first page, bent closer and began to study it.

"What is it?" Dan rasped.

The priest held up his hand. "Wait!" he ordered.

Dan stepped back a pace. Father John, face wrinkled in concentration, continued to pour over the parchment. Presently he lifted his hand. "This," he said slowly, "is the record of a Spanish court. It is the report of a suit between Don Silberio de la Luz and Don Portillos Alarid."

"What does it say?" Dan demanded. Gotleib was beside the priest now, bending down, peering over the priest's shoulder, his thin face keen and excited.

"I'll read it for you," Father John announced. "It will be slow, for the writing is old and hard for me to read. Sit down. I'll read it."

CHAPTER SIXTEEN:
GOOD WINE SPEAKS

Fitzpatrick's bartender, opening up at nine o'clock, wakened Vicente. The bartender had come down early, and he was pleased to find his guest still asleep. Jack had relayed Fitzpatrick's instructions to the bartender, including the warning not to leave Vicente alone.

Awake, stiff from his long ride and still very weary, Vicente stayed around the saloon, hoping for something that would help him. He felt alone, discarded and out of the picture. Dan Shea, the bartender told him, was at El Puerto del Sol. He advised Vicente to get out there because Martin O'Connor was being buried. There was definite hostility in the attitude of the bartender who, as he often announced, didn't like a Mexican. Vicente sensed that hostility and reacted to it typically. It was as natural as breathing for Vicente to take a full quart of wine when the bartender's back was turned.

With the quart hidden under his coat Vicente fared out to see what he could do about breakfast and transportation to El Puerto del Sol. East of the plaza, in that section of Bendición that was known as Chihuahua, Vicente encountered a friend, one of

the men from the shearing crew in which Vicente
had acted as *colero*. Vicente gave his friend a drink,
and the friend gave Vicente breakfast at his house.
Warmed and satisfied by the meal, Vicente forgot
his determination to get to El Puerto. He decided to
stay in town awhile.

Vicente's friend was filled with news. From the
friend Vicente learned of the things that had occurred in Bendición since his departure for the
north. Too, in all the native population of the town,
there was an undercurrent of rumor. Talk and
speculation were rife concerning El Puerto del Sol
and the death of Don Martin O'Connor. There was
a story circulating, a nebulous tale that had no facts
to back it, that there had been a big fight and that
O'Connor and Salvador Ocano had been killed
during the combat. Vicente, his friend, and some
others that came in polished off the bottle. Vicente
had money given him by Dan Shea. Basking in his
glory as a returned traveler, as a man who had seen
far places and come back, and as an Indian fighter,
Vicente bought a fresh supply of wine.

The news of Dan Shea's return was spread over
Bendición. Jack, who had carried word to Fitzpatrick's bartender, told the story when he visited the
post office. The bartender amplified the tale when
he was questioned. Dan Shea was back and had
gone directly to El Puerto del Sol. Vicente Lebya
had been with Shea, the bartender said. Vicente
was someplace around town. It was very natural
that George Delaney, coming down to get the
mail, should hear the story. It was natural, too,
that Delaney should be worried. From the post office he went directly to his law office where he
kindled a fire in his small sheet-iron stove. Then as

the fire warmed the room Delaney sat down behind his desk and, the mail forgotten, indulged in thought.

Delaney was afraid of Dan Shea. In all his conniving and scheming, Dan had been the unforeseen factor, the one person that Delaney could not discount. Somewhere in his plans, Delaney knew, things had gone wrong. There had been a mistake, a grave blunder, else Dan Shea would never have returned to Bendición. George Delaney was frightened. A frightened man commits errors. George Delaney sent for Ramon de la Luz.

It was eleven o'clock before Ramon answered the summons. Arturo was with Ramon when he came into Delaney's office. Ramon was anxious, for Delaney's summons had been urgent. Arturo swaggered as he came through the door and, finding a chair, placed his hat on the floor beside him. Since the death of Martin O'Connor Arturo had felt his importance keenly. He played the *bravo* whenever he was in Bendición.

"Dan Shea is back," Delaney announced without preamble and looking steadily at Ramon. "He came in last night."

Ramon took some of Delaney's alarm to himself. His eyes were bright and questioning as he looked at Delaney.

"¿ Es verdad?" he queried.

Delaney nodded. He was fluent in Spanish, more accustomed to that language than Ramon was to English. Still, adept as he was, Delaney could not easily find words for what he wanted to say.

"Is he in town?" Ramon asked.

Delaney shook his head. "He went out to El Puerto del Sol last night. Fitzpatrick took him."

Ramon, now that he thought about it, could not see anything very dangerous in Dan Shea's return. He saw that Delaney was alarmed, and that fact naturally made him nervous; but not being informed of all the facts that Delaney had, Ramon was not so concerned as his friend. "Shea went out to the funeral?" Ramon asked.

Delaney grunted. "There's a man in town who came back with Shea," he announced. "I'd like to find out what Shea's going to do."

That was reasonable enough, from Ramon's viewpoint. He looked at Arturo. Delaney had the same idea. He also looked at Arturo. "Maybe you could find out," Delaney said.

Arturo, already filled with his own importance, took on a greater stature in his own mind. He nodded importantly.

"This man's around town someplace," Delaney said. "You hunt him up, Arturo. Find out what he knows, and then come back here."

Arturo picked up his hat. "I'll do that," he agreed.

"And don't get into trouble," Delaney warned. "Just find out about Shea if you can."

Arturo swaggered out, closing the door importantly, and Delaney straightened in his chair and drummed on the desk top.

"Why are you worried about Shea?" Ramon demanded suddenly. "Can he do anything?"

"I don't know what he can do," Delaney returned. "He wasn't supposed to get back here at all. I thought I had him stopped."

Ramon lounged back in his chair and began fashioning a cigarette. Dan Shea did not seem particularly important to Ramon. "Have you heard when the suit is to be tried?" he asked, moistening the flap.

"This spring," Delaney answered absently. "I wonder how Shea got back. I wonder if he found out anything."

Ramon lit the cigarette. At the moment Ramon was sure of himself and of everything else. Now that Martin O'Connor was dead Ramon felt certain that soon he would be a wealthy man in possession of most of El Puerto del Sol and of a great deal of money. He basked in his anticipated wealth. Delaney had assured Ramon that there was no chance of losing the suit, that all things would go just as he, George Delaney, prophesied. Ramon let smoke trickle from his nostrils and looked at Delaney with mild amusement.

"Shea can do nothing," he announced. "I have a just suit against El Puerto del Sol. I will win it. Then you will not need to worry about Shea, *amigo mió.*"

George Delaney made his second mistake then. Harassed and worried, sudden anger welled up in him, anger with Ramon, so self-confident, smoking so nonchalantly. "A just suit!" Delaney snapped. "I made that suit for you. If Dan Shea found out . . ."

Ramon dropped the cigarette and straightened in surprise. "Found out what?" he demanded. "What could he find out? About O'Connor, you mean?"

Delaney nodded. "You don't know Dan Shea," he said morosely. "If he knew how O'Connor was killed he'd kill us both."

Ramon ground out the cigarette beneath his boot sole. He stared at Delaney. "Kill us?" he questioned.

Delaney nodded. "Quick," he agreed.

A little glow of fright came into Ramon's eyes. "Then . . ." he began.

"That's what I think," Delaney interrupted. "I think we'd better do something about Dan Shea. I thought I had him taken care of, but something slipped."

"How?" Ramon was leaning forward in his chair.

"I sent Tom Warms and Buster Flint up north to see that Shea didn't get back," Delaney rasped. "He got by them someplace."

For a long moment Ramon said nothing, and Delaney, rising from his chair, took a short turn across the room. "I'm not going to have Shea butt into this again," he announced suddenly, facing Ramon. "Not when I've got this far with it. Not when I planned the whole thing."

Ramon shook his head obstinately. "He can do nothing," Ramon announced positively. "My suit will be settled and I will win. I am not afraid."

Pent-up wrath possessed George Delaney. Ramon was so sure, so certain of his position, so impregnable. Delaney had a sudden impulse to shake that sublime self-certainty. "You're not afraid!" he rasped. "You sit there talking about winning your suit and what you're going to do! Let me tell you, you haven't any suit. I fixed it up. It was I who saw the chance and took it!"

"What do you mean?" Ramon half arose from his chair and sank back once more.

Delaney had said too much, or not enough. He had to go on. Crossing to his desk again, he sat down. "I mean that there was already an adjudication on that land," he snapped. "I mean that if it weren't for me you'd be out with a little bunch of sheep, herding them. I saw the chance and took it; that's what I mean!"

Ramon shrank in his chair, seeming to grow smaller. Delaney, having begun, could not stop. Words poured from him as water from a fountain.

"I was in Santa Fe going through some records and I found the file on El Puerto del Sol. I saw where there'd been a suit against the grant by some of your folks and how it had been settled by the Spanish. It looked like a chance. I got Maples to take that file from the records and I talked you into starting suit. Maples got wise and tried to black-mail me and I hired Tom Warms to kill him. Warms didn't get the file. That damned Shea was there and took a hand, and Tom and the others just barely got away. Shea killed one of them. I don't know what's become of the papers. They're around some-place. Suppose that file turned up? Then what would become of your suit?"

Ramon de la Luz sat huddled in his chair, his eyes fixed on Delaney's flushed, excited face.

"Shea took a bunch of sheep north and sold them so that there'd be money to fight the case," Delaney continued. "And now he's back. He got by Warms and Buster. If he found out about what I'd done he'd kill me. You too!" Delaney glared at Ramon de la Luz. Again Delaney sprang out of his chair and paced across the office. Close by the door he whirled and confronted Ramon.

"Don't you breathe a word of this!" he snarled. "You're in it too. If they get me they get you, you understand that? Everything I've done, you've done too. They wouldn't believe you if you tried to tell them different!"

Dumbly Ramon nodded. Delaney strode back to

the desk and stopped. "By God," he snarled, "I'll get rid of Dan Shea! I'll do it myself. I won't trust any more bunglers!"

The good wine warmed and strengthened Vicente Lebya, helping him to forget his weariness. Friends were about him and would remain so long as he had money and was willing to spend it. This was a far different Vicente from the lad who had been a *colero* with the shearing outfit. Vicente was broader and taller, and on his cheeks and chin curled the fine growth of new-grown beard. His clothing might be worn and ragged, but inside the rags stood a man. A fine fellow!

As the morning grew older more friends joined the gathering. In winter, with no work to do, the Mexican population of Bendición was avid for entertainment. Vicente afforded it. He bought wine and he talked of his adventures, enlarging upon them. The tale of the fight with the White Mountain Apaches was repeated and repeated, improving with each telling. In his friend's house Vicente leaned back against the wall, tipping his stool, and held up his right hand. The Señor Shea and Vicente were just so. Vicente held two fingers close together. They were one. About him those who listened and drank sighed their admiration.

There was another tale to tell, Vicente hinted. Not one that he could speak of at the moment, but later, perhaps. . . . Vicente nodded significantly, his very silence forecasting great things. A new group pushed through the door and joined the party. Vicente, flushed with wine and with his triumph, looked into the scarred, saturnine face of Arturo de la Luz.

Not six months before Vicente had been afraid of Arturo. But many things had happened in six months. For many days Vicente had eaten all that he could hold. He had grown. His beard had sprouted. He had been Dan Shea's shadow and, more than all these, Vicente had been matched against men and he had won. Arturo held no terror for him now. He grinned and waved his hand in invitation toward the wine on the table.

Arturo and the two men with him helped themselves to the wine and sat down. Vicente, called upon again to tell the tale of the Apaches, launched into the story. By now it was a trifle old to most of his hearers. Vicente, sensing their indifference, sketched his story lightly. Having finished it and failing to see the desired impression, Vicente spoke further.

"That was not all," he continued. "El Señor Shea and I were attacked as we returned."

"Attacked?"

Vicente nodded solemnly. He had promised Dan Shea, promised faithfully, that he would not speak of the attempt made upon them below Bernalillo. Dan wanted no complications with the sheriff's office in Albuquerque, no delay on his journey to Bendición and, accordingly, had warned Vicente to silence. But Vicente was Indian, Apache all the way through. His tale of the Indian fight, through repetition, had fallen flat. There was a letdown in his heroism. It was more than the boy could do to refrain from braggadocio.

"Two men," he boasted. "El Señor Shea carried gold in his belt. These two men attacked us at night when we were coming from Bernalillo. Señor Shea was ahead and I followed. They called to us, and Señor Shea stopped. He was taken by surprise, but not I. I had my gun. I raised it so." Vicente demonstrated. "Then . . . bang! . . . bang!" (Vicente failed to mention that the old Springfield was a single shot.) ". . . and one man went down. The other ran, but I had my knife. I caught him!" Vicente looked carefully about the circle to see that the desired impression was created. Satisfied, he made his final statement.

"He did not run far," Vicente concluded significantly.

"With the knife, hah?" The owner of the house peered at his guest. "You caught him and used the knife?"

Vicente shrugged. "What would you have done?" he answered. "It was his life or mine."

Arturo leaned forward. "This man, this *ladrón*, he talked to you before he died?" Arturo asked.

It made a good tale. Vicente shrugged once more. "Like a dying sinner to a priest," he agreed. "He begged for his life. He told me many things."

Arturo leaned back and sipped the wine. Vicente did not speak further concerning the confession of the man he had killed. There had been no confession, and Vicente was not inventor enough to build one from his imagination.

"What does Señor Shea intend?" Arturo asked, mindful of his errand.

Vicente waved his hand. In that gesture, more plainly than any words he could have spoken, he conveyed the impression that Dan Shea had consulted with him as a familiar, seeking advice. "What would you?" Vicente answered. "He will marry la

Señorita O'Connor. Naturally he will take up Don Martin's quarrel."

"He knows the men who killed Don Martin?" Arturo was leaning forward.

Vicente stared at Arturo, shrugged and lifted his eyebrows. Wordlessly Vicente conveyed the impression that Dan Shea had the answer to that question and that he, Vicente, also had the answer. Arturo stirred nervously.

"So . . ." The man who owned the house let the word go in one long breath. "More wine, *amigo?*"

"*Con mucho gusto,*" Vicente agreed.

There was a disturbance outside the house. A small boy, appearing at the door, made shrill announcement. "*¡Los pastores! ¡Mira, papa! A quiestán los pastore's del Señor Shea.*"

The men about Vicente flocked to the doorway, Vicente with them. It was true. Outside the house were Hilario Bargas and Nopomencenco and Cercencio and the rest. Vicente advanced to greet them.

Both the men and their animals showed the wear and tear of their journey. The men were bearded, their clothing tattered and their bodies shrunken into the rawhide toughness that hard and protracted travel brings. The mules they rode were also gaunt and worn but, like the riders, toughened by the trail. Behind Nopomencenco's saddle there was a pair of gunny sacks tied together and slung across the mule's quarters. From one sack a dog's head protruded. Bravo, the puppy that Vicente had found in the ruined *placita,* was returning to El Puerto del Sol, coming back with his rescuers. Weaned, but as yet too young to make all the journey on foot as had the other dogs, Bravo was riding. As Vicente advanced Bravo bared his sharp little milk teeth and snarled a warning.

"Bravo!" Vicente exclaimed, and then he was beside the mule, reaching up and grinning.

Hilario, Nopomencenco, Cercencio, all were dismounting, climbing down from their mounts. There was a babble of voices, and in that confusion, while men were greeting men and friend was shrilly calling to friend, Arturo de la Luz slipped away.

Arturo went directly to Delaney's office and pushed in. Delaney and Ramon had come to an end in the talking. Delaney had thought himself into a state of fright and desperation. Ramon was even more frightened and equally desperate. It had been borne home to Ramon de la Luz that he was an unwitting tool for Delaney but that, unwitting though he might have been, he was equally involved. And Delaney had not forgotten to impress on Ramon that it was Ramon who first shot Martin O'Connor. Somehow Delaney made that appear to be the major crime, and not the two deliberate shots that had followed and put an end to O'Connor's life.

"What did you learn?" Delaney demanded as Arturo slammed into the room.

Arturo had closed the door and stood leaning against it. He was sweating, although the day was cold. "I listened to Vicente," Arturo answered, the words tumbling out. "Shea knows who killed Don Martin."

Blank silence followed that statement. Then Delaney snapped: "Are you sure?"

"Sure." Arturo nodded with conviction. "I listened to everything Vicente had to say. By Bernalillo two men attacked Señor Shea. He killed them both. Vicente killed one with a knife. He said that the man he killed begged for his life."

Delaney sank back into his chair and stared blankly at Ramon. "Tom Warms and Buster Flint," he said, his voice hoarse. "I told them . . ." Delaney stopped. Ramon still sat huddled in his chair.

"What will we do, Ramon?" Delaney said. "We've got to do something!"

Ramon made no answer. Delaney's voice was shrill. "You're in this too. Don't forget that! Say something. We've got to do something!"

In the big living room of El Puerto del Sol Father John finished his reading. The small echo of his voice hung in the silence for an instant and then was gone. Gotleib, stirring in his chair, reached out, and the priest placed the parchments in the little lawyer's hand.

"That settles it!" The lawyer's voice held his triumph. "They haven't a leg to stand on. If the case comes to trial I can present these and . . ." He broke off and looked at the others. They were not, Gotleib realized, interested in the legal victory that was in his hands. Dan Shea was grimly quiet; Louder contemplated his clenched hands; Perrier studied the toe of his boot, and Fitzpatrick was staring out the window again. It was borne to Bruno Gotleib that legalities were not in their minds. These men were considering other, grimmer things.

"I wonder how Maples come to have 'em," Fitzpatrick drawled, not turning from the window. "He was killed on account of them, you know."

"Yes," Dan agreed quietly. "That's the reason Delaney had him killed."

"Maples?" Gotleib inquired. "I knew . . ."

"Maples ran a little abstract office in the capital," Fitzpatrick informed. "Dan an' I were there when he was murdered at San Felice."

Gotleib looked from the lanky saloon man to Dan and then back again. He rubbed his hand against his bearded cheek. "Maples," he murmured once more. "I heard something about that. I don't remember . . ."

Dan did not enlighten the lawyer. He was watching Fitzpatrick, and his voice came slowly as he spoke his thoughts. "Maples would have had access to the files in the land office because of his abstract business, and no one would have been suspicious of him. Likely Delaney hired him to steal this"— Dan's hand indicated the parchments that Gotleib held—"out of there. Then Maples wouldn't turn them over to Delaney. That must have been the way of it."

"That's likely it," Fitzpatrick agreed. "So Delaney hired him killed." Fitzpatrick had turned from the window to watch Dan Shea as Dan talked.

"So then," Dan's voice went on without inflection, "this Lucero who was hostler at San Felice stole Maples' grip. Lucero went back to the reservation. Why he saved these papers no one will ever know, but he did save them. He got in with a bunch of young bucks at the reservation, started out on a raid with them and met up with us. Lucero got killed, and Vicente got his pack, and now we've got the stuff that Maples stole."

Fitzpatrick and Louder nodded slowly. Dan's explanation was logical, reasonable, perfectly plausible and possible. "Go on, Shea," Louder ordered. "Tell the rest of it."

Dan's eyes sought Louder's. "Why, yes," he agreed. "I can tell the rest. It was Delaney. He figured this out from the start. He hired Maples to get the only proof that El Puerto del Sol really belonged to O'Connor. He wanted it in his hands. Maples double-crossed him so Maples was killed, and still Delaney didn't get what he wanted. He went ahead anyhow. He had the suit started. He knew I'd seen him with one of the men that killed Maples, so he sent that man to kill me. You chased him off, Louder. Remember?"

Louder nodded. "Git on with it," he commanded gruffly.

Dan tipped his chair back and then let the legs strike the floor again with a little thump. "Delaney tied up Don Martin's money. When I took a herd north and sold it he hired Buster Flint and this same man who had killed Maples to lay for Vicente and me. And . . ." Dan's voice trailed off into silence.

"And what?" Louder snapped.

"And it was George Delaney who killed Don Martin," Dan concluded.

"Ain't you forgettin' Ramon?" Fitzpatrick asked.

"Ramon de la Luz hasn't brains enough to figure a thing like this. It was Delaney! Delaney used Ramon."

Silence followed that assertion. Gotleib rolled the parchments so that they crackled in his hands. Fitzpatrick, Perrier, Louder and Father John eyed Dan. "You have no proof of this, my son," Father John said gently.

Dan turned to Gotleib. "You said," he reminded, "that Delaney and Ramon de la Luz were in Albuquerque two days before Don Martin's body was found."

Gotleib nodded. "That proves nothing, of course," he interposed quickly. "Legally . . ."

Slow anger rose in Dan Shea, hot and high and quick as a flame. "Legally!" he snarled. "Legally! Are you asking me to sit back and wait until I can prove this legally when I *know*?"

Gotleib shook his head. Perrier, rising, came over to stand beside Dan. Some of the Englishman's reticence was stripped from him. His nut-brown face showed excitement. "I'm with you, you know," he told Dan Shea.

Dan did not look at Perrier. Somehow he had known that this slight sportsman would be beside him in whatever he did. Father John's eyes were troubled, and Gotleib was staring unseeingly at the papers he held in his hand.

"So?" Fitzpatrick prompted.

"So"—Dan's voice was very low—"I'm going into Bendición and throw what I know into George Delaney's face!"

Silence followed that statement. Louder got up and shook himself. His words were very prosaic and matter-of-fact. "There's lots of folks around Bendición," Louder stated, "who will side Ramon de la Luz. Some that will stand by Delaney too." Fitzpatrick was nodding gravely. The lanky cowman paid no attention to the saloonkeeper. "I'm goin' to the ranch," he announced. "I'll be back by daybreak with the boys. *I* was named in that suit too. Don't forget that, Shea!" Picking up his hat, Louder started for the door. At the door he paused. "I'd take it mighty unkindly if you was to go without me." The door opened and closed behind the cow-man's shambling figure.

"He's right, you know," Fitzpatrick reminded when Louder's boot heels had ceased to sound on the porch. "There's lots of folks that will side Ramon de la Luz and George Delaney. Lots of them!"

CHAPTER SEVENTEEN:
HOUNDS TO THE KILL

Sam Youtsey, sheriff of Seco County, knew that he was sitting on a powder keg. The sensation was far from restful. Since early morning Youtsey had watched his town of Bendición fill up with the hard-eyed adherents of Ramon de la Luz. Since early morning he had sought to learn the cause of the influx. His efforts had brought some results. Questioned as to why all his kinfolk were in town, old Tio Abrán de la Luz had shrugged his shoulders and given a partial answer. He understood, Tio Abrán said, that there was to be some trouble over the suit against Martin O'Connor. Ramon had sent out and asked him to come in. With that information Tio Abrán had borrowed papers and tobacco, rolled a cigarette and, forgetting to return the tobacco, walked away from Youtsey.

Sheriff Youtsey sought Ramon. He did not find the head of the De la Luz clan. Ramon was nowhere in evidence, and inquiry failed to locate him. Sam Youtsey gave up the search. There were many De la Luzes, many votes. Sam Youtsey wished to keep in the good graces of those voters. In his office in the courthouse he sat at his desk and consulted with his two deputies, Manuel Torres and Bert Cassidy.

Manuel was placid. There were almost as many Torres as there were De la Luzes and, come what might, Manuel was pretty sure of his deputy's appointment.

"Some trouble, I hear," Manuel said, answering Youtsey's question. "The De la Luzes do not like El Puerto del Sol for a long time back. I theenk eet ees over that."

"I know they didn't like O'Connor," Youtsey snapped. "But he's dead. They ain't got no cause to fight now."

"Theese Señor Shea, he ees not dead," Manuel commented. "Mebbe so they weel fight weeth heem."

Youtsey grunted. Manuel was a weak staff upon which to lean. The sheriff turned to his other deputy. "What's your idea on this, Bert?" he demanded.

Bert Cassidy shifted his chew of tobacco. "You might," he suggested, "throw Ramon's pants in the can. If you done that Ramon wouldn't make no trouble."

"Hell!" Youtsey exploded. "No trouble!" He stared balefully at his husky deputy. "That's what you know about it! Where would I be next election if I done that?"

"Out of a job," Bert answered promptly. "You could arrest Shea if it come to that. You didn't get no votes from El Puerto last time, anyhow."

Youtsey brightened. "I *could* do that, couldn't I?" he said. "You ain't so dumb, Bert. You stay here an' look after things. Manuel an' me 'll ride out the bridge road an' see what's happenin'. Come on, Manuel."

Manuel shrugged placidly and bestirred himself. "*Si,*" he agreed.

"You might change your mind about it," Bert warned as Youtsey moved toward the door. "That bunch of sheepherders that went north with Shea was in town last night. They all had rifles, an' they pulled out for El Puerto just as soon as they found out about O'Connor."

Youtsey hesitated a moment. There was a lot in what Bert Cassidy said. Then happy inspiration seized the sheriff. "I'm goin' out, anyhow," he announced. "There was some sheep stole up the river, an' Manuel an' me 'll go look into it. You hold down the office, Bert. I got confidence in you. Yo're responsible." With that the sheriff pushed open the door. "Come on, Manuel," he ordered.

The sheriff tramped on out. Manuel smiled gently at Bert whom he did not like. "Adiós, amigo mío," said Manuel and followed his boss out into the hallway. Bert, his plug of tobacco halfway to his mouth, stared at the empty doorway. Then, angrily, he slammed the plug down on the floor. "Can you beat that?" Bert Cassidy demanded.

Out of the courthouse, en route to the livery barn, Sam Youtsey got a good view of what he was leaving behind him. In the plaza, assembled on its corners, were little clumps of men. They looked warily at Youtsey as he passed them by. Not a man that was not armed, not a man that was not in some manner connected with the clan of De la Luz. At a rough estimate, and Youtsey's estimate was not only rough but hurried, there were some extra adherents of Ramon scattered around the plaza. Youtsey, with Manuel shuffling along half a pace in the rear, did not pause for accurate counting or for words. He went to the livery barn.

"Lots of folks in town, Sheriff," the hostler commented as he moved along the barn alley to the stall where the officer kept his horse. "Seems like there's lots of people. It ain't Saturday, is it?"

"No," Youtsey answered. "It ain't Saturday."

The hostler brought out the sheriff's mount. Manuel was rustling his own horse. "Headin' out, Sheriff?" the hostler asked.

"Been some sheep stolen up north," Youtsey answered. "I'm goin' out to look into it."

The hostler said, "Oh," reflectively and cleaned off the horse's back with his brush.

"Hurry up," Youtsey commanded. "I want to get out there."

"Yeah," the hostler agreed and kept on cleaning the horse.

When finally he reached the outskirts of the town Youtsey was in a lather of impatience. The two horses walked across the bridge, their feet sounding hollowly on the planking. They pulled up the hill beyond the bridge, making for the mesa top where the roads forked. As they topped the rise the two, sheriff and deputy, stopped their horses. There, coming down the road toward them, was a small army. Mounted men, riding in irregular squadrons, filled the road. There were nearly a hundred of them, and in the van where—so they believed—it was their right to be, immediately following Dan Shea and the other leaders, were the ten riders from the YH. There was no mistaking their identity. Nonchalant, insouciant, devil-may-care, the cow hands of the YH were coming in company with their traditional enemies, the sheepmen of El Puerto del Sol.

"Gawd!" Youtsey breathed. "Look at that!"

Manuel stared but said nothing. It was too late to retreat. From the front of that marching column four men detached themselves and came loping toward the sheriff and his deputy: Dan Shea, Jesse Louder, Fitzpatrick and Perrier. They drew rein as they reached their goal and Louder, looking sternly at Youtsey, made inquiry. "Where you headed, Sheriff?"

Youtsey cast aside all attempt at subterfuge. For once he spoke the truth, point-blank. "I'm gettin' out of town," he said. "There's an army waitin' in there for you."

Louder looked significantly at Dan Shea. "How many?" he asked quietly.

"I don't know. There's fifty or sixty around the square." Youtsey was sweating freely.

"I think mebbe you'd better go back," Louder growled. "After all, yo're the sheriff."

"I ain't goin' back," Youtsey said defiantly. "I'm not goin' into the mess that you folks 'll make. Not me."

"Let him go," Dan ordered. "We won't need him. Is there a deputy in town?"

"Bert Cassidy's there. You can get him if you want an officer."

Louder and Fitzpatrick looked at Shea expectantly. "They're waitin' for us," Dan drawled, paying no attention to Youtsey. "Well . . ."

"Well?"

Dan looked at the officer. "You go along, Youtsey," he said, his voice not unkind. "Just high-tail it over the hill. Don't head back to Bendición. That's all I ask."

"I ain't goin' back there." Youtsey vowed. "Not now."

"Then ride out."

Youtsey pulled his horse to the left and, with Manuel, headed north. Dan Shea, Louder, Fitzpatrick and Perrier watched him go.

"That's why I was against him last election," Fitzpatrick stated. "No guts."

"But he did us a favor," Dan reminded. "He told us what there was waiting for us in Bendición."

"Are we goin' in?" Louder demanded.

"That's where we started."

"But if they're waitin' for us . . ."

"We'll do it just a little differently," Dan interrupted Louder. "You said that you were in this, Jesse."

"I am, but I don't want my boys to ride into an ambush. I . . ."

"I don't think they will," Dan interrupted once more. "Youtsey said the De la Luzes were waiting for us. Will they be waiting for you and your boys and Fitzpatrick?"

"No," Louder answered, puzzled. "I don't think so."

An appreciative grin formed on Fitzpatrick's face. Dan Shea smiled grimly. "If you went to town," he said, "and kind of posted yourselves where it would do the most good, it looks to me like we could dodge a lot of trouble. I don't want to kill men that have nothing to do with this. I don't want to kill anybody. All I want to do is to throw what I know in Delaney's face."

Louder pushed back his hat. With knotted brown fingers he scratched his gray hair. "I could put about four men on each corner," he said. "Before anything started they could get the drop. Shea, yo're smart."

"It ain't no wonder you Yanks beat us," Fitzpatrick chuckled. "Yore smart tricks would take in anybody. How do we do this an' when do we go?"

"I'll tell you," Dan Shea said.

With Perrier's dogs lying in the dust, watching their master with adoring brown eyes, the four men held consultation. Then, in couples, they rode back to the waiting army. Dan Shea called Hilario to him. Hilario listened while orders were given. He nodded agreement and then, with Cercencio and Nopomencenco, trotted off toward the bridge. After perhaps ten minutes three others of the herders who had accompanied Dan on the long drive followed Hilario and his companions.

"That's all for now," Dan informed Louder. "We can't send too many."

Louder nodded. "When do you want me to go?" he asked.

"Pretty soon now. We'll let Fitz and Perrier go in first."

"That would be better," Fitzpatrick agreed.

The men from El Puerto del Sol, under Dan's instructions, left the road, secreting themselves in the brushy draws close by it. Fitzpatrick and Perrier talked together. Louder, joining his riders, dismounted and entered into discussion with his men. Dan Shea stood apart by himself, looking at the road, at the river and the bridge and not seeing them. He was thinking about El Puerto del Sol.

Gotleib was at El Puerto. The little lawyer had wanted to come but, obedient to Dan's wishes, had remained at the ranch. Marillita also was at El Puerto del Sol. Worn out with her long vigil beside her father's bier, weak from the sudden shock she had suffered, Marillita—Dan hoped—was resting.

Obedient as a weary child, at Dan's suggestion she had gone to bed, and while Dan Shea and his friends sat in grave consultation, Marillita slept.

During the consultation Hilario, Vicente and the herders arrived. To them Dan Shea had confided something of what he knew, something of the plans that had been made. He could trust these men. Long months of close association had bound them to him. They were his men and, equally, he was their leader.

Roused momentarily from his meditation, Dan glanced down beside him. Vicente squatted there, his bright black eyes fixed upon Dan Shea.

"I go with you, Señor Dan?" Vicente asked.

"You go with me," Dan assured.

Vicente smiled. Dan's eyes grew moody once more. Again he retired into his thoughts. It was all right, Dan thought. Gotleib and Father John would see Marillita through no matter what happened to him, Dan Shea. Gotleib had the evidence. Gotleib would work and fight, if necessary, and assure Marillita of continued possession of El Puerto del Sol. The priest would comfort her. El Puerto del Sol! It was bigger than Marillita, than Dan Shea, bigger than them all and more demanding. Martin O'Connor had made El Puerto del Sol, and Martin O'Connor was dead. Salvador Ocano had been born on El Puerto, and Salvador had spent his life in the service of the place. He, too, was gone. Dan Shea marveled a little at those things. El Puerto del Sol was a possession; it was owned, and yet in the final analysis it was El Puerto del Sol that was the possessor, the owner, the master of them all.

"We're goin' now, Dan," Fitzpatrick announced. "Perrier and me."

"Good luck, Fitz," Dan answered.

They rode away, Perrier on his great bay horse, his dogs following. Dan glanced at his own mount. He was riding one of Perrier's horses, the big Wellington he had ridden on that hunt so long ago. Fitzpatrick and Perrier! El Puerto del Sol had swept them up just as it had gathered in himself, Dan Shea. Momentarily Shea thought about the Englishman. What lay behind Perrier? he wondered. And why was Perrier riding off with Fitzpatrick? Because of Dan Shea? Men and dogs dropped from sight over the hill. Dan's thoughts returned to Marillita.

She knew nothing of this venture. The expedition had been organized while she slept. While Marillita rested El Puerto del Sol gathered itself to strike back at the men who menaced it. To Dan Shea, waiting there, it seemed almost as though El Puerto assumed a personality. El Puerto del Sol became a monster demanding homage, service and finally revenge.

Louder came strolling over from his men. "Who's goin' with you, Shea?" he demanded.

"Vicente," Dan answered.

Louder grunted and eyed Vicente speculatively. "I hope this works," he said. "I sure hope it does."

"You needn't go in," Dan said quickly.

"Hell!" Louder spat into the road. "Who said anything about not goin' in? I declared myself, didn't I? I anted, didn't I? Damn it, Shea, I got as much stake in this game as you have."

"You'd better go then," Dan answered calmly. "It's time."

"All right," Louder agreed. He walked over to his horse and, mounting, spoke cheerfully. "Come on,

boys." All about Jesse Louder his men rose into
their saddles. They rode away with a small, swag-
gering clatter. Dan watched them go and then,
walking back along the road, spoke to the men
who rose up to meet him.

"You will stay here," he ordered. "I will go to
town presently, but you will stay here."

Young Pete Ocano, Salvador's son, spat into the
sand. "*Sí*, Señor Shea," he agreed. "We will stay
here . . . unless something happens."

Perforce Dan let it go at that. So far he was in
control, but behind him was El Puerto del Sol, and
El Puerto del Sol might wrest the control from him.
These men were El Puerto del Sol, and Pete Ocano's succinct words spoke their mind. Dan had not
wanted them to come, but they had come. Now
they would remain under his command unless, as
Pete said, "something happened." Dan nodded and
went back to his horse and Vicente. The next move
was in his own hands. After that . . .

"We go now, Vicente," Dan Shea said.

About the plaza in Bendición men stirred. Beyond
the plaza, in the outskirts of the town, Hilario Bargas and Cercencio and Nopomencenco distributed
themselves, guarding the outskirts. Hilario stood
at the door of a friend's house, talking, and Cercencio and Nopomencenco waited at the corner of the
house, watching the street. At the entrance of another alleyway three more of Dan Shea's herders
lounged, the focusing point for many curious eyes.
From a house a man slipped away and walked toward the plaza, bearing the word that the herders
were in town.

In the doorway of Fitzpatrick's saloon Fitzpatrick

himself stood talking to Perrier. Perrier's dogs were lying in the street, and great Mab held the bridle reins of Perrier's horse in her mouth.

"About time," Fitzpatrick murmured, and Perrier nodded agreement.

Debouching upon the plaza, coming along the street that led to the bridge, a compact group of riders trotted, Jesse Louder in the lead. They stopped their horses at a hitch rail and, dismounting, tied their animals. With many a tug at chaps or gun belts, they separated, spreading about the square, talking and laughing together, splitting up into pairs, each man, seemingly, with a chosen companion. The YH had come to town. The pairs of men strolled around the plaza and, somehow, without apparent design or objective, located themselves upon the four corners of the square.

Up in the courthouse Bert Cassidy threw his chew into a cuspidor, latched a belt about his middle and jerked down his hat. "Damned pup," grated Cassidy, speaking of his boss, "runnin' out on me! There ain't goin' to be no trouble! I'm goin' out."

In George Delaney's office Delaney peered through a crack between the window shade and window frame. "Louder has come to town," Delaney said to Ramon de la Luz. "I just saw him pass."

"I think . . ." Ramon began.

"I don't like it," Delaney snapped. "I wonder where Shea is."

"He isn't coming," Ramon announced. Ramon, having fortified himself with whisky from Delaney's bottle, felt brave and confident.

"You don't know Dan Shea!" Delaney retorted. "He . . . I'm going out back a minute, Ramon."

Dan Shea, on big, white-stockinged Wellington,

had ridden into the plaza. Vicente was behind him, looking back. George Delaney waited no longer. He had seen Louder's men distributed about the square. He knew what was coming. Delaney walked past Ramon, not hurrying, apparently at ease. He opened the back door, stepped out and closed it; then he hurried his pace. Down in the alley, in a shed, there was a saddled horse.

With Delaney gone, Ramon went to the window. He peeped cautiously out. The plaza was strangely quiet. There was no movement. To Ramon's dazed eyes the scene presented itself. On the corners men stood frozen, motionless as statues. Ramon saw the reason for the quiet. There, where they could command, Louder's riders stood, and in the hands of each man was a pistol, a heavy gun that menaced the small knots of Ramon de la Luz's followers, that enforced the peace and the quiet. Dan Shea's strategy was in operation, and, coming along the sidewalk with Vicente a step behind him, was Dan Shea.

"Delaney!" Ramon shrilled. "He's come. Shea is here."

There was no answer. Ramon turned and, running to the back door, threw it open. The alley was empty.

"Delaney!" Ramon's voice was high and filled with fright. "Delaney!"

Dan Shea, coming along the sidewalk, saw Fitzpatrick and Perrier leave the door of the saloon and come toward him. From a distance there sounded the muffled roll of thunder and, for an instant, amazed at the sound, Dan stopped. Then realizing that the thunder was the pound of many hoofs crossing the bridge, Dan came on. Pete Ocano had not waited for "something to happen." He was bringing the men of El Puerto del Sol on into town.

Dan reached the door of Delaney's office, turned the knob and threw the door open. For a moment, standing there, he could not see the details of the interior. The shades were drawn and the room darkened. Then, his eyes adjusted to the light, Dan stepped in. Behind him, the doorway instantly filled, Vicente, Perrier and Fitzpatrick crowding through. Perforce Dan moved to let them enter. The room was deserted and the back door was open.

"Delaney!" Dan rasped and ran toward the back door.

As he reached it there was a shot in the alley. Adobe chipped from beside the door, and Fitzpatrick's broad hand against Dan's back sent him reeling to sprawl in the alleyway. A shrill voice screamed: "No! No!" and rolling, scrambling up, Dan halted, resting on one knee. Ramon de la Luz was cowered against an adobe wall across the alley, and Fitzpatrick, legs widespread, arm extended, was leveling his long-barreled gun.

"No!" Ramon screamed again. "No!"

"No, Fitz!" Dan seconded Ramon.

The gun in Fitzpatrick's hand came level and poised. The hammer was back, and Fitzpatrick's finger was on the trigger, but the hammer did not fall. Dan came on up to his feet. Ramon's hands were lifted, and his weapon lay in the dust beside the adobe wall.

"Where's Delaney?" Dan rasped. "Where is he?"

In his panic Ramon could not answer. He could only babble words, pleadings for his life. Fitzpatrick lowered the gun and, striding across the alley, jerked Ramon to his feet.

"Where's Delaney?" Dan rasped again.

"Delaney's run!" Fitzpatrick grated. "Got away."

Dan ran toward the end of the alley. It was empty. The street likewise was deserted. Fitzpatrick had hauled Ramon into Delaney's office, was standing over him. Louder was at the door.

Dan Shea burst through the back entrance to the office. "He got away," Dan Shea raged. "Delaney's got away. I'll catch him."

Pushing past Louder, he crossed the office at a run and was out upon the street. The plaza was ominously quiet. Men from El Puerto del Sol, reinforcing Louder's riders, occupied it. There was a buggy just rounding into the plaza, Gotlieb driving, Marillita wedged between the lawyer and Father John. Dan did not see the buggy. He ran on toward his horse, jerked the reins free and flung himself into the saddle. Perrier was running from Delaney's office, calling to Mab, the hound; and Mab, still holding the reins of Perrier's horse, came in answer to the call, the horse trotting after her. Dan's horse reared, came down and pounded along the side of the plaza. Perrier mounted, wheeled his bay and followed Dan. At the corner the Englishman reined in and, bending low, called to a wide-eyed boy who stood there.

"Which way did Delaney go?"

The boy pointed toward the north. Perrier, straightening, pounded after Dan Shea, overtaking him.

"North!" Perrier shouted. "He went north!"

At the intersection Dan turned his horse, obeying that shout from behind. Following Perrier, the four dogs—Mab and Puck and their two fellows—loped easily.

The riders went through the outskirts of the town, clearing the buildings. There were a few scattered adobes and then open country, the road stretching away like a ribbon toward the north, following the river valley. Dan reined in and waited for Perrier to come up. Far ahead where the road climbed to surmount a rise of ground, a horse and rider, miniatures in that sweep of country, appeared momentarily. Wordlessly Dan Shea started his horse ahead, breaking from walk to run in three great bounds. Perrier, a part of his mount, followed. They pounded down the road, the dust gouting up from the thundering hoofs.

Atop the rise, with the width of the valley before them, they saw the dot of running horse and rider once more. Delaney was fleeing, making the most of opportunity. Dan Shea kept on, but Perrier, reining in, called sharply. "Puck! Here, Puck!"

Perrier thrust out one stirruped boot. Puck came at command, as trained, reared, resting his forepaws upon the outthrust boot.

"There, Puck! There!" Perrier pointed with his crop. "Hie on. Hie on, Puck!"

There was no wolf, no coyote that Puck could see. He looked up at his master questioningly.

"Hie on, Puck. There. Hie on!"

The dog discerned the moving dot of horse and rider. Trained to the chase, obedient, he dropped down and swept away, and behind him came Mab and the others. Great bodies close to the earth, legs scissoring, fanged heads outthrust, they swept past Dan Shea, and behind them Perrier's big hunter ate into the distance.

So intent was Dan's gaze upon the man ahead that he hardly saw the dogs go past. Delaney's horse was running, covering country. Beyond Delaney the road, dropping to the bottom land, entered the brush, the thick growth along the river. If Delaney reached that hiding he might escape, and Delaney was closing the distance between himself and safety. And then Dan saw the dogs running low, cutting into the space between himself and his quarry, effortlessly, soundlessly.

It was Mab that first reached Delaney. A wolf, she would have closed with instantly and pulled down. But this was no wolf; this was a man on horseback. For the first time Mab gave tongue and Puck, coming up, added his roaring voice. Delaney's horse, frightened, bucked viciously as he ran and swerved away from the four-legged peril. Unseated, Delaney toppled, strove for control, lost it, kicked his stirrups free and fell heavily. About him the dogs ringed themselves, panting, waiting for their master. Dan Shea slid his horse to a stop as Delaney scrambled to his feet. The dogs, their tongues lolling, not knowing what was expected of them, waited. Dan dropped from his saddle, took two swift steps and confronted the man he had pursued.

Delaney's wild eyes sought an avenue of escape; noting the dogs, they then fixed themselves upon Dan Shea. Dan stood, regaining his breath, facing George Delaney. "It was you!" Dan accused. "You, Delaney!"

Perrier had reached them and, stopping his horse, dismounted, in at the kill.

"God damn you, Shea!" Delaney screamed. "Damn you!" His pistol, whipped from his belt, swung up level and exploded. Dan Shea felt the shock of the slug, reeled, caught his balance. Mab reared up, barking furiously. Puck was crouched, ready to spring. Almost as though this were a picture, Dan Shea saw all this: the dogs, Delaney's wild eyes, his leveled gun. Then without volition, seemingly, his own weapon was out. He felt the sharp recoil against the fork of his hand, saw Delaney's arm drop, and then the dogs were in and Perrier was shouting:

"Mab! Back, Mab! Down, Puck! Down!" and, crop swinging, was among the snarling tangle of hairy bodies. Dan Shea groped behind him for support, touched a sweaty shoulder and leaned back against his horse. The world swam before him, and in the swimming world Perrier whipped the dogs away.

CHAPTER EIGHTEEN:
TOMORROW

When the dogs were at last quiet, when they lay in the dust, their tongues lolling, Perrier came to Dan. Blood dripped from Dan's fingers, and his shoulder was afire. The little brown-faced man offered aid, baring the shoulder, wadding a clean handkerchief against the wound and binding it there. Dan hardly knew that he was being aided. He was sick, sick of heart, sick of body and of mind. Reaction had set in, and the anger that had driven him was drained away, leaving him weak.

Perrier seemed to sense the sickness and the weakness. His voice, clipped and brittle, penetrated to Dan, whipping his mind back to life. "You had it to do," Perrier snapped. "You gave him a sporting chance. You had it to do!"

Dan made no answer. He looked past Perrier to where Delaney lay, inert, in the road. Perrier interposed his body between Dan and the dead man and spoke again.

"I tell you, you had to do it!" There was anger in Perrier's voice, as though he were irked by Dan's seeming failure to understand. "My God, man! What else was there for you? Look here, Shea!"

Reluctantly Dan turned his eyes until they met
Perrier's. Perrier's blue eyes were bright and shin-
ing; his brown face was firm. "You can thank your
luck that it isn't you," Perrier snapped. "He tried to
kill you."

"But . . ." Dan began.

"And you can be thankful that she'll understand." Perrier's voice softened. "You did it for her.
Marillita will know that!"

It was true in a measure, this thing that Esme
Perrier said. Marillita would understand, and in a
way George Delaney lay there in the dust because
of Marillita. Dan realized that. But only part of
what Perrier had said was true. There were other,
larger things. Dan Shea caught hold of himself,
forced his mind back to sanity. Delaney was dead,
killed by Dan's hand. All the moil and trouble that
had engulfed El Puerto del Sol was finished, and
the man that had caused it was gone, forever
through with his plotting. But . . .

"I wasn't so fortunate," Perrier said slowly, his
eyes averted from Dan's face. "No. I wasn't so fortunate." He turned, staring up the road toward
Bendición.

Sharp in Dan Shea's mind the words cut. Here
then was a partial explanation of Esme Perrier.
Somewhere behind the little brown-faced rider was
a tragedy. Somewhere in his past was a woman who
had failed to understand, who had been unable to
perceive the force that made Esme Perrier what he
was. That explained Perrier, explained his presence
and his mode of living. Shaken as he was, Dan's
sympathy went out to his companion. He half raised
his uninjured arm, reaching out toward Perrier.

Perrier did not see the movement. "They're coming out from town," he announced. "They're almost here."

Dan turned toward the south. Not two hundred yards away Louder's foreman and three men from El Puerto del Sol were riding. Just behind the foreman was Vicente.

They left the two from El Puerto to stay with George Delaney until a wagon could be sent out for the body. Vicente and Perrier helped Dan into his saddle, and he sat there quietly while Perrier gave the orders. Then Vicente, Perrier and Louder's foreman mounted, and Perrier brought his horse up beside Dan Shea's mount. So, without looking back, they took the road to Bendición.

When the men reached Bendición the little town had calmed noticeably. True, there were still knots of armed men assembled on the corners. True, the men who had come from the YH and El Puerto del Sol patrolled the streets. But there was a lessening of tension apparent. Fitzpatrick met Dan Shea and Perrier as they entered the plaza. He took one look at Dan and ordered them to follow him. Close beside Delaney's office Fitzpatrick stopped and, coming up to Dan, helped him to dismount.

"Doc's inside," Fitzpatrick said.

Dan Shea allowed himself to be led into the doctor's office. Somehow he sensed, without being told, that things were under control. Fitzpatrick helped the doctor strip off Dan's coat, shirt and undershirt. They sat down in the chair, and the doctor, a chuffy little man with thick glasses, made an examination.

"Nice clean hole," the doctor commented. "Went right through under the shoulder. Hmmm. Didn't touch the bone. Lucky. Hmmm. Well, young man . . ."

The doctor's monologue was interrupted by the precipitous entrance of Marillita. The girl made straight for Dan and flung her arms about him, dropping to her knees upon the floor so that she could better reach him. Her tears were wet against his cheek, and her mouth soft against his own, and her arms were fiercely tender. After that first embrace she drew off, just so that her arms were not so tight, and she talked, her voice at once tender and fierce, happy and sad, reproachful and proud. She chided Dan Shea and she praised Dan Shea, and Dan, drawing her close with his good arm, kissed her again and stilled her flow of words, and the doctor puffed and hovered about anxiously and demanded that he be allowed to attend his patient. Finally the doctor's voice broke in upon them, and Marillita got to her feet.

The chuffy little man swathed shoulder and chest in bandage, muttering all the while. He fastened the bandage in place and informed Dan Shea that he was lucky and to come back to see him tomorrow. Dan heard not a word that the doctor said. He was looking at Marillita, and his eyes glistened. As soon as the doctor had done Marillita took possession of her man once more. She was helping Dan on with his shirt, at the same time telling him how she had forced Father John and Bruno Gotleib to bring her to Bendición, when Fitzpatrick made his appearance.

"Pretty near through, Dan?" Fitzpatrick asked. "They want you in Delaney's office."

Marillita buttoned Dan's shirt over his arm which swung in a sling the doctor had improvised. She helped Dan on with his coat and then, taking his arm possessively, she went with him out of the office.

Delaney's office was crowded. Louder was there, and Gotleib. Perrier stood just inside the door. Bert Cassidy was standing, wide-legged, looking down at the pale-faced Ramon de la Luz. Old Tio Abrán was beside his nephew. Arturo occupied a chair in a corner of the room, very small indeed, with Vicente poised before him. Vicente had his hand upon the haft of the knife in his belt, and Arturo's eyes were fixed with dreadful fascination upon that hand.

"I wanted you to hear this, Dan," Bruno Gotleib said curtly. "Ramon!"

As though his name were a cue, Ramon spoke. His voice was flat, with the monotony of fear in it. Like a gramophone with a weak spring and an old needle, Ramon entered upon his recitation. His tale was complete. Twice during its telling Marillita swayed and found support in Dan's strong arm. Once when Ramon spoke of the murder in the goat-herder's rock house the girl murmured pitifully. But when Dan Shea suggested that she go Marillita strengthened. She was beside Dan. She would spend the rest of her life beside Dan Shea.

"So that's it," Gotleib said, his lean face keen as he looked at Dan when Ramon's recital was completed. "That's all of it. Delaney had planned everything, from stealing the file at Santa Fe right on through. He hired Maples killed and he killed Don Martin."

Dan Shea nodded soberly. Over beside the door Perrier's voice sounded loud in the silence which followed Gotleib's words. "Good dog, Mab," Perrier said. "Good dog, Puck." The men in the room turned toward that voice. Mab and Puck were standing in the door, their great heads just inside the room. Puck opened his mouth so that the mighty fangs were exposed, and he yawned as a dog sometimes will when pleased. Dan's arm tightened about Marillita.

Then Tio Abrán had his word to say. Tio Abrán, all through his nephew's recital, had stood, a statue carved from mahogany and clothed as a man. His small black eyes under their white brows never left Ramon's face all through the story. When Ramon was done Tio Abrán moved forward and spoke.

"*¡Cobarde!*" Tio Abrán snapped, and then even more scornfully: "*¡Tonto!* Fool!" With that he turned abruptly and stalked toward the door. Louder made a move to interpose, but Fitzpatrick said sharply: "Let him go!"

Louder stepped back and Tio Abrán went on out to the street. Momentarily he stopped and then, turning sharply to the right, approached a group of his adherents. Standing in the office door, Fitzpatrick and Louder watched the old man.

It was plain that Tio Abrán de la Luz was telling his listeners what had occurred. Neither man in the doorway could hear the words, but they could see expressions and gestures. It was evident at first that Tio Abrán's listeners were incredulous; then as he continued to talk their expressions changed. Tio Abrán made a spreading gesture with his arms as though scattering his kinfolk, lowered his arms and waited.

"What's he doin'?" Louder demanded. "Is he . . . ?"

"Tio Abrán," Fitzpatrick drawled, "is a dead-game

sport. He knows when he's backed a losin' hand. Watch! They're breakin' up."

Indeed it was true. About the old man his listeners were dispersing. Some, with sullen glances toward the men in the doorway, started across the street, making toward the wagons tied there; others, their voices shrill as they spoke of what they had heard, moved along the sidewalk, stopping to talk to those of their faction that they met. Tio Abrán·was one of these. At the hitch rack a man untied a team, climbed stiffly into a wagon and backed it out.

"Why," Louder said, "they're pullin' out. They're done."

"Sure," Fitzpatrick agreed. "Tio Abrán's spreading the news. He hates a coward. I think this is finished, Louder."

"Just the same," Louder announced grimly, "I'll let the boys hold things down awhile longer. There might be some that get ideas."

Fitzpatrick turned back into the office. Louder remained at the door watching the plaza. Other wagons were departing now, and all along the plaza sides the little knots of De la Luz adherents were breaking up. With a grunt Louder left the doorway.

"That's that," he announced with finality.

As Louder left the door Bert Cassidy made his announcement. Cassidy, who had been a spectator in the drama, now assumed a role. "I guess I might as well take Ramon an' Arturo to jail," Cassidy remarked. "That's about all there's left to do."

"You want some help?" Louder asked.

Cassidy glanced from Arturo to Ramon and then looked at Louder. The deputy was chewing again, his jaws moving rhythmically on his cud. "No," he answered calmly. "I guess not. Git up, Arturo. Come on, Ramon."

Arturo got up, still cringing from Vicente. Like a man in a daze Ramon de la Luz obeyed the deputy's command. Cassidy reached out a hand on either side, drawing his prisoners together. "Go on," he commanded and, a pace behind the two, started them toward the doorway. Just at the door Cassidy paused. "I'll look after Delaney," he announced to the room at large, "just as soon as I get these fellers located. You needn't to bother about it." Then Bert Cassidy went out, following his unresisting prisoners.

When the door was cleared Fitzpatrick looked at Dan Shea and then all around at those left in the office. "By gosh," Fitzpatrick announced positively, "there goes the next sheriff as far as I'm concerned. I'm goin' to back him. He's all right."

Louder was nodding agreement. Dan Shea stared at the empty doorway. Fitzpatrick, having endorsed Bert Cassidy, spoke again. "What you goin' to do now, Dan? Go to the hotel? You can't get back to El Puerto tonight. It's already gettin' dark."

The tension was gone now. Dan Shea's nerves sagged, and weariness possessed him. "I guess that's right, Fitz," he said. "I guess we'll go to the hotel."

They left the little office then, the office where George Delaney had studied and plotted and acted against El Puerto del Sol and, issuing from its door, they saw the plaza. Jesse Louder's riders still occupied their vantage points, but there was no more need for them. The plaza was emptying. Wagons creaked away. Riders, some scowling, some with uncertainty in their eyes, followed along the streets, heading toward the exits. Dan Shea walked slowly, Marillita beside him, Fitzpatrick flanking his other side, Gotleib and Louder striding ahead and Vicente and Perrier bringing up the rear.

"I guess the boys can turn loose now," Louder commented and, breaking away from Gotleib, approached his foreman on the corner. Dan Shea did not see this, did not see the foreman's sudden grin or his quick departure after Louder's words. Dan Shea was looking at Marillita. He was not thinking of Louder or of Louder's men or of Fitzpatrick striding along before him or of Perrier and Vicente walking alertly behind.

Hilario and Nopomencenco, with others of the herders following them, came along the side of the plaza, approaching Dan's party. Hilario started forward toward Dan Shea, but Nopomencenco caught his arm and drew him back. Hilario wanted orders and had come for them, but Nopomencenco, having glimpsed Dan's face, knew that the orders must wait.

"*No importa,*" Nopomencenco said, and Hilario, having also looked into Dan's eyes, obeyed the hand upon his arm and stopped his advance. Orders were not important.

"I'll start to Albuquerque tomorrow," Gotleib informed Louder who had rejoined him. "When I get there I'll amend our answer to the suit. I'll take that decision with me and get it back to the land office."

"Yeah," Louder agreed. He was watching his men, all of them, gathering in front of Fitzpatrick's saloon. They would go into Fitzpatrick's and get a drink and then another drink. By the time they finished they'd be feeling plenty high. He ought to . . . Louder grunted aloud, interrupting his own thoughts. Those were all good boys he had, and the foreman was with them. They wouldn't get too drunk, and if they did what difference did it make? Those boys had sided him right straight through, and if they wanted to drink a little liquor it was all right.

Fitzpatrick, too, was watching the group gathering in front of his saloon. Plenty of business tonight, Fitzpatrick thought. Maybe he ought to get back to the place. His bartender was all right, but maybe just a little too handy around the till. As soon as he got Dan located he'd go over to the saloon. He'd buy all those boys a drink or two. They'd earned it.

Perrier, following along behind, looked at Dan Shea's back. It was broad and flat and his hips were slim: a proper back for a horseman. Perrier's blue eyes gleamed. There was a man to ride with him, a man who asked no quarter and gave none. A thoroughgoing sportsman! Against Perrier's hand great Puck pushed his head, and Mab, jealous, came up on the other side, thrusting herself between her master and Vicente. Absently Perrier touched Puck's head. Absently, with the fingers of the other hand, he found Mab's silky ear and caressed it.

Vicente, too, was watching Dan Shea's back. There was adoration in Vicente's eyes. As Mab and Puck followed Perrier, so Vicente followed Dan Shea, unreasoning, willing, loyal. There, in front of Vicente, walked his *patrón*, the master.

Marillita, looking up into Dan's face, saw that his eyes were blank. He was looking at her and not seeing her. "Dan," Marillita said softly.

With a start Dan Shea returned to the present. He had been far away. Wandering.

They had stopped now, all of them. The hotel was before them, and Louder and Gotleib, Perrier and Vicente, were gathered around.

"Tomorrow," Dan Shea said, "we'll go back to El Puerto del Sol." He looked at Marillita as he spoke, excluding all the rest, locking them out.

Marillita met that look fully, fairly, bravely. Watching those two, the others stood a moment and then, as though aware that this was a tryst, a meeting in which they had no part, turned away their eyes.

"Tomorrow," Marillita promised. "Tomorrow, Dan."

The last of the sunlight, coming across the plaza of Bendición, filtering through the leafless cottonwoods, casting the shadows long before it, caught and tangled in Marillita's hair and gleamed like gold.

The Classic Film Collection

The Searchers by Alan LeMay

Hailed as one of the greatest American films, *The Searchers*, directed by John Ford and starring John Wayne, has had a direct influence on the works of Martin Scorsese, Steven Spielberg, and many others. Its gorgeous cinematic scope and deeply nuanced characters have proven timeless. And now available for the first time in decades is the powerful novel that inspired this iconic movie.

Destry Rides Again by Max Brand

Made in 1939, the Golden Year of Hollywood, *Destry Rides Again* helped launch Jimmy Stewart's career and made Marlene Dietrich an American icon. Now available for the first time in decades is the novel that inspired this much-loved movie.

The Man from Laramie by T. T. Flynn

In its original publication, *The Man from Laramie* had more than half a million copies in print. Shortly thereafter, it became one of the most recognized of the Anthony Mann/Jimmy Stewart collaborations, known for darker films with morally complex characters. Now the novel upon which this classic movie was based is once again available—for the first time in more than fifty years.

The Unforgiven by Alan LeMay

In this epic American novel, which served as the basis for the classic film directed by John Huston and starring Burt Lancaster and Audrey Hepburn, a family is torn apart when an old enemy starts a vicious rumor that sets the range aflame. Don't miss the powerful novel that inspired the film the *Motion Picture Herald* calls "an absorbing and compelling drama of epic proportions."

KENT CONWELL

"A great read. Be prepared for adventure."
—*Roundup* on *Chimney of Gold*

As the moon rises, the night riders come out, sweeping over ranches in the valley, bringing fear and intimidation. Someone wants the owners to sell—badly—but like a few other holdouts, Ben Elliott has sworn not to give up his land for any price. So the night riders have upped the stakes. Once they were content to rustle cattle, but now they've moved up to killing livestock…and murdering men. There's only so much a decent man can take. Ben Elliott has reached that point. It's time for him to fight back. It's time for the nights of terror to become…

Days of Vengeance

ISBN 13: 978-0-8439-6226-0

COVERING THE OLD WEST FROM COVER TO COVER.

Since 1953 we have been helping preserve the American West
with great original photos, true stories, new facts,
old facts and current events.

True West Magazine
We Make the Old West Addictive.

TrueWestMagazine.com
1-888-687-1881

Based on the immortal hero from the bestselling
Riders of the Purple Sage!

ZANE GREY'S™ LASSITER

BROTHER GUN

JACK SLADE

Lassiter, the solitary hero from Zane Grey's *Riders of the Purple Sage*, became one of the greatest Western legends of all time. Now America's favorite roughrider is back in further adventures filled with gun-slinging action and rawhide-tough characters.

BLOOD BROTHER

Lassiter owed Miguel Aleman for saving his life. To repay the favor, he swears to protect Miguel's troublesome son Juanito. He never thought he'd have to make good on his oath so soon, though. When Juanito kills a horse trader in a drunken brawl, he faces the gallows—unless Lassiter can save him. But the only option Lassiter has is to break the law himself...which might very well leave him swinging right along with his blood brother.

ISBN 13: 978-0-8439-6238-3

☐ **YES!**

Sign me up for the Leisure Western Book Club and send my FREE BOOKS! If I choose to stay in the club, I will pay only $14.00* each month, a savings of $9.96!

NAME: _____

ADDRESS: _____

TELEPHONE: _____

EMAIL: _____

☐ I want to pay by credit card.

☐ **VISA**   ☐ **MasterCard**   ☐ **DISCOVER**

ACCOUNT #: _____

EXPIRATION DATE: _____

SIGNATURE: _____

Mail this page along with $2.00 shipping and handling to:
Leisure Western Book Club
PO Box 6640
Wayne, PA 19087
Or fax (must include credit card information) to:
610-995-9274
You can also sign up online at **www.dorchesterpub.com**.
*Plus $2.00 for shipping. Offer open to residents of the U.S. and Canada only.
Canadian residents please call 1-800-481-9191 for pricing information.
If under 18, a parent or guardian must sign. Terms, prices and conditions subject to
change. Subscription subject to acceptance. Dorchester Publishing reserves the right
to reject any order or cancel any subscription.